FILTHY JOBS AND STEAMY SHOWERS

Mucky Men Doing Dirty Work

PETER SCHUTES

ADAM MAXWELL BIGGLESWORTH

CONTENTS

LIFT PUMP

1. Meet Gerry   3
2. Lunch With the Fellas   13
3. Submission   16
4. Broken Pump   24
5. A Lift Home   32
6. Crystal and Beer   35
7. Happy Ending   42

WEE DOBBIN   55
by Peter Schutes

DARK AS A DUNGEON

1. Shorty   73
2. Moose And His Friends   82
3. Priscilla's Rebuff   94
4. A New Opportunity   100
5. Dropping The Soap   105
6. Cumberland Gap   109
7. True Detective   123
8. Earl   127
   Epilogue   136

About the Authors   139
Other Books from Peter Schutes
Publishing   141

LIFT PUMP

by Adam Maxwell Bigglesworth

MEET GERRY

Gerry worked at the Oceanside Wastewater Treatment Facility in San Francisco. All the sinks, showers, baths, and toilets west of Twin Peaks, including the Sunset and Richmond Districts, flowed to Gerry's work. There were 25 million gallons a day of wastewater, 35% of which was solid waste. Most of the solid waste was "organic debris," as they liked to call it, but a portion of it was inorganic: plastic, rubber, cloth, and thick paper - all the things that San Franciscans were asked not to flush, but they did. The plant used a box screener to force the solid human waste into a sludge, separating out the inorganic debris.

It was a disgusting, smelly, and dangerous place to work, but the pay was good, and Gerry could afford to own a house in the Castro District. He was gay. As far as he knew, none of his coworkers were gay. They talked about pussy and tail and gave Gerry a wide berth because they knew he wasn't into that. It was a bit lonely, but he had a fondness for alone time. His job as a tester gave him lots of time alone in the laboratory. He measured the PH and bacteria levels of the water before it was pumped four miles out to sea. As long as the water was 95% clean, it was good enough for the ocean.

Gerry's lab had an air filter that removed most of

the unpleasant odors, but once in a while, it got pretty bad. The smell would permeate his clothes and stick to his skin. On those days, he had to take a shower before catching the streetcar home. The shower room was just an open row of shower heads; no dividers, no curtains. He dreaded those days. He was self-conscious about his enormous cock, at least at work. Straight guys were brutal. The other guys had seen it. They gave him nicknames like "Ass Smasher" and "Gerry the Fairy with a Dick So Scary." He knew they were probably jealous of his massive endowment, but he didn't like the attention and teasing one bit. His coworkers didn't appreciate him like the queens in the Castro did.

Gerry had one friend at work. Lex was a tester who sometimes shared the lab with Gerry. He was quiet, reserved, and never gave Gerry any shit about his cock or his queerness. Lex had curly, dirty blond hair and pale blue eyes. His half-smile looked good in a white lab coat. He wore a wedding ring. Gerry treasured their friendship. Lex had a dry sense of humor, and he always gave Gerry a good laugh whenever he did speak up. Their quiet companionship was exactly what Gerry needed at work. They both had a shy demeanor. He knew Lex appreciated him.

Gerry wasn't shy when it came to hunting for sex in the bars and gyms. Gay boys would see the outline of his soft bulge in his tight jeans, and follow him home like he was the Pied Piper. He loved fucking ass. He was at the top end of really big: too big for a lot of guys, but a dream come true for a real loose queen. He'd fuck them and send them home limping. He never let a trick stay the night. As mentioned, he liked being alone.

Being so big, he'd had his share of rejection. A lot of greedy, inexperienced queens would get back to his house and chicken out when he pulled it out semi-hard. If they stuck around long enough to see it rock hard, they'd usually leave. A few of them would beg him to let them suck it, but they could only lick the tip. If Gerry was horny enough, that was okay. But fucking ass was what made him horniest of all, and sometimes he sent them home and went back out for new prey.

Gerry loved a muscular bottom. He had the tool to lure them. He spent time at the gym in the Castro, half-heartedly working out before getting naked in the hot tub. He didn't like working out, but the bodybuilders didn't seem to mind his flab. They saw his cock and went hog wild. Sitting in the whirlpool, his cock would float to the surface. Eyes popped, asses twitched.

San Francisco was a small town at heart, but it had a lot of visitors, so Gerry never had to fuck the same ass twice. The dickmatized queens would beg for a second chance, and if he was feeling generous, he might do them a few times, particularly if their ass and body was muscular. Something about seeing his massive cock disappearing between dimpled, round butt cheeks made him come quicker. If they had big hard man tits, he'd hold them by the chest, and that cut the time in half again. He wasn't into a long, slow fuck, but sometimes he had no choice. Being so big, it could take a long time to come if he wasn't as turned on.

One Sunday, he walked on the treadmill, his cock swinging in his sweatpants. There were a dozen men eying him and whispering, but he'd been with all but one. The doe-eyed newcomer was his quarry for the day. He stepped off the treadmill and approached the muscular youth.

Gerry said, "You like what you see?"

The boy had black hair and green eyes, with a thin dusting of hair on his shoulders and back. A furry muscle boy with a big ass was a triple-turn-on. Gerry felt his cock swelling just looking at him.

The boy blushed. "Uh, it looks pretty big."

"It is."

A long silence ensued. The boy's eyes were locked on Gerry's crotch. "Is it really that big?"

Gerry laughed. "Come take a shower and I'll show you."

The boy was a real lifter. His biceps bulged and his ass was eating his shorts. Gerry knew he could fuck a guy like him because he'd have a high tolerance for pain. He obediently followed Gerry to the shower room.

Gerry stripped, his semi swinging between his thighs, halfway to his knees. The kid was hesitant to take off his clothes. Was he going to be a perfect four? Gerry loved guys with tiny dicks.

"What's your name, kid?"

"Charlie Lowell." As he said it, he pulled his shorts out from between his ass cheeks and lowered them, revealing a mostly empty jock strap. Gerry's cock surged at the sight. Charlie took a step back, astonished at the size.

"Holy shit."

Gerry grinned with confidence. "You think you could handle something like this?"

Charlie lowered his jock strap, revealing a thumb-sized cock in a nest of black pubic hair. "I think so. Maybe."

Gerry said, "Come on, look at you. All muscle. You're no stranger to pain. No pain, no gain."

Charlie gulped, eyes wide with a mixture of fear, greed, and lust. His tiny cock stood at attention. "I don't think it's a good idea to do anything here."

Gerry agreed. "We can go back to my pad. It's a block from here."

He watched as the little fur ball debated the pros and cons. He loved that moment when they gave in. It came slowly, but it came.

"Yeah, alright. I wanna try it."

They showered, dressed, and left the cruisy gym. A few broken-hearted former tricks stared glumly. A couple of others whispered, giving Charlie nasty looks. They were consumed with jealousy. Gerry didn't give a fuck. He wanted what he wanted, and he had the equipment to get it.

Back at Gerry's apartment, he took the lead. He undid Charlie's belt and pulled down his jeans. Charlie kicked off his sneakers and stepped out. Next, Gerry unbuttoned his shirt and took it off. He put a hand over the boy's jockstrap and gently rubbed it. Charlie wriggled with delight.

"You still wanna let me fuck you?" Gerry always checked. He didn't want some stupid fag accusing him of rape.

Charlie nodded. He started to remove his jockstrap.

"No, leave it on for now." Gerry knew he'd come too fast if he saw the kid's tiny penis dribbling from the pressure of the big cock in his ass.

Gerry had a tub of Crisco by his bed. He scooped up a big glob and rubbed it up and down his cock. It glistened in the sunlight that shone through the cracks in his curtains. He dipped a forefinger in the shortening and scooped up a generous helping.

"Spread your cheeks."

Charlie put one hand on either mound of muscle and spread them apart, revealing a pink, hairy hole. Gerry's cock dripped in anticipation, but he had to be patient. Carefully, he spread the shortening over the opening, then inserted his index finger. The boy didn't flinch. Good. It wasn't his first time at the circus.

Gently, Gerry inserted his middle finger, sliding in and out before twisting it. The hole gave easily. This boy was loose. Perfect.

He put in his ring finger and formed a triangle. The boy winced, then relaxed. "Mmm. That feels good."

Gerry appreciated the compliment. His fingers were pretty big. Some stupid queens chickened out at this point, but not Charlie. He forced his thumb and pinky into the hole, spreading his fingers apart.

Charlie pounded the dresser, causing the mirror to creak. "Oh, shit! Don't! Stop!"

Gerry waited, but couldn't resist a joke. "Did you say 'don't stop?'" He chuckled at his own joke.

Charlie panted, speaking between breaths. "Just. Wait. There. Please."

Gerry knew he needed to let the boy adapt. His hole was loose, but not the kind accustomed to fisting. The five fingers, when stretched apart, were nearly as big around as Gerry's cock. He liked to get his knuckles past the hole at least once. That would be a little bigger around than him. It was the final test before he switched gears.

After a full minute, Charlie groaned. "Okay, pull it out a bit and go back in."

Gerry had done this hundreds of times. It was an old routine. He loved fucking a loose hole, and this was the way to get what he wanted. He punched gently, pushing a little further each time, until his knuckles finally broke past the ring.

Charlie shuddered. "Do it. Put it in."

Gerry couldn't believe his luck. This boy wanted him to fist him. It was not the first time, but exceedingly rare. He obliged. Charlie let out a holler, then his hole clamped down around Gerry's wrist.

"Oh fuck. Oh god! Your wrist is so thick. Shit! Oh, shit!"

Gerry made a fist and tried to pull out, but Charlie cried out. "Not yet."

Gerry knew better than to ignore a boy with a fist up his ass. He also knew that this was going to be a really good fuck when they got started. Fisting was not his favorite. Shooting his load up a muscle butt was the only thing that satisfied his hunger.

"I'm coming out now. There's some poppers right there."

Charlie grabbed the little bottle of amyl and snorted heavily.

"Okay."

With a slurping sound, Gerry pulled out, satisfied with the fur-lined, red, gaping hole he'd made in the boy's backside. His cock throbbed, itching to fill it.

"I think you're ready now. Bring that amyl with you."

Gerry lay on his bed, his knees hanging over the edge. His giant cock towered above him, throbbing with anticipation.

Charlie straddled Gerry's waist, facing him, his feet firmly planted on the hard mattress. His short legs needed only to bend 45 degrees in order for the massive cock to rest against his hole. He held a nostril and took a massive sniff from the bottle, squatting down. With an audible pop, Gerry's head slipped inside.

Charlie shuddered and swooned. "Oh, fuck. You're gonna split me in two, aren't you?"

Gerry chuckled. "Hasn't happened yet. Take your time." In truth, he wanted that hot muscle boy to sit in his lap so he could start fucking him, but he knew patience was in order.

Charlie took another whiff and bent his knees to a 90-degree angle. Gerry felt his head bump the back of the rectum. Charlie straightened and bent his knees, letting the first five or six inches of Gerry's cock fill him and empty him out.

"I don't think I can go any further." Charlie looked down and shook his head ruefully. "Is that good enough?"

"Hold on. I got a surprise. Take another hit and sit as far as you can."

Charlie sniffed the bottle, a puzzled expression on his face. Gerry loved this part. As Charlie sat down,

Gerry grabbed his waist, twisting it to the left. He found the second hole and pulled Charlie down to his lap. The boy's eyes rolled back in his head. After about thirty seconds, he came around.

"Oh, fuck! What was that?" Charlie was a second-hole virgin. Thankfully, that hole isn't a real muscle; even a dick as big as Gerry's slips right past with nothing but a loud pop.

Charlie sat in Gerry's lap, his mouth like a fish out of water, gasping and closing.

Gerry held the muscle boy by the waist and flipped him onto his back. Now Gerry was on top, where he liked it.

"You ready to see paradise?"

The boy nodded, a little fear on his face, but no grimace of pain.

Gerry began his rhythmic fucking. He started with short strokes, keeping his cock buried in the boy's colon. After a minute, he pulled out further, so that the inside hole gave another pop, then pushed back in. Pop!

Charlie took another whiff of poppers as Gerry sped up, taking longer strokes. Pop! Pop! Pop!

"Jesus, that feels good!" Charlie thrashed back and forth in ecstasy. He cried out enthusiastically, "Don't stop!"

Gerry couldn't resist. "You want me to stop?"

Charlie shook his head violently. "No. Don't stop."

"No. Don't. Stop?"

"Keep going for fuck's sake!" Charlie joined Gerry in laughter.

Gerry was a great ass-fucker. He took long, fast strokes, sending Charlie into spasms. He bucked and thrashed. His hole gave up trying to squeeze shut; Gerry could slide in and out without resistance. So he did. Faster and faster, he pummeled the hairy boy's ass, the hairs tickling his shaft.

Charlie pulled aside the jockstrap to reveal his little

dick, dripping with precum. "I gotta come. I don't want to get it dirty."

Gerry saw the little throbbing cock, and it pushed him to the edge of the precipice. Under the fur, he saw Charlie's abdominal muscles contracting involuntarily. It was all too much. He knew he was past that point. He didn't want to stop.

Charlie said, "Fuck, oh fuck." Without touching himself, Charlie shot a massive load onto Gerry's belly, then his own furry chest. The warm cum trickled and dripped. It was the final straw.

"Oh, kid, you're gonna get it now. I'm coming."

"Do it! Shoot your load."

Charlie cupped the boy's rock-hard ass cheeks, lifting him slightly off the bed so he could fuck harder. His balls churned. It was time.

"Oh, fuck! Oh, sweet Jesus. I'm coming!" Gerry pulled the boy's ass cheeks hard; his hips ground against them. A warm sensation came flooding up the inside of his shaft. Deep inside the boy, he shot a massive load. His balls contracted, and his cock throbbed like a bee stinger. He pumped a dozen times before the contractions ceased.

They stayed locked together. Charlie tried to kiss Gerry, but he wouldn't let him. Kisses were too close. He didn't want any attachment to the boy. Charlie's eyes watered but no tears came. Gerry hated that hurt expression.

With a slurping wet sound, he pulled out of the boy, bringing a small tide of semen with him. The rest was buried far up inside the kid.

"That was great." Gerry wiped his cock clean and put on his boxer shorts. The head of his limp cock hung below the cuff, as always. He wished there were some underwear for a guy as big as him, but there wasn't. He couldn't possibly wear Fruit of the Loom or BVDs. Lost in thought about undergarments, he forgot the muscular youth was in his bed.

"Should I go?" Charlie's voice woke Gerry from his reverie.

"Yeah, that would be great. Thanks for a great time."

Charlie frowned when Gerry tossed him a towel to wipe up. "Yeah, thanks, too. I guess. Can we do it again?"

Gerry shook his head. "I prefer not."

Charlie dressed and left the apartment in a huff. Gerry didn't give a shit. He didn't want any entanglements. Or so he thought.

LUNCH WITH THE FELLAS

The next day at the sewage treatment plant, some of the guys invited him out to lunch. They wouldn't take 'no' for an answer. There was a nearby Doggie Diner that had a walk-up window and outdoor tables. The guys couldn't go into a regular restaurant smelling like they did. Gerry sat quietly, listening to the other guys swap stories about pussy. Lex didn't join in. Judging by his wedding ring, he wasn't single like them. Gerry figured he didn't have any wild sexcapades to share with this horny bunch of heteros. Gerry debated telling the story of Charlie just to see the look of shock on their face.

Bruno, a particularly ugly sonofabitch, could tell Gerry was debating it. "Gerry's got a story, I can tell. Come on, Gerry, tell us about one of your queer fucks."

Gerry was sick of it. He decided to shock them all.

"This hot bodybuilder at the gym came back to my place yesterday and I fucked the shit out of him."

The table roared with laughter. It wasn't mean. They were startled and delighted.

"Go on," Lex said. Gerry was surprised this shy married man wanted to hear anything about his sex life.

Gerry thought *fuck it. Just give these motherfuckers the whole story.*

He said, "He was short, with a lot of fur, the way I like them. He was all muscle."

Bruno leaned in like he wanted to hear more. "Who fucked who?"

Gerry snorted. "I fucked him, like I said."

Bruno said, "The poor guy. Can he walk?"

Gerry said, "If you keep interrupting, I ain't telling you shit."

"Sorry, keep going."

Gerry continued. "He was staring at my crotch at the gym." For emphasis, Gerry grabbed his meat through his work pants.

Hal, a barrel-chested furball gasped. "Shit, that's big."

Bruno said, "You just noticed?"

Hal blushed.

Gerry said, "That's it. I'm done. Eat your fuckin' hot dogs."

Bruno put a hand on his shoulder. "I'm sorry, bro. I'm sorry. I'll shut up. Please, go on. You've had to listen to our bullshit for years. It's your turn."

Gerry sighed. "So I get him home, and he's got this tiny little dick. The way I like them."

Lex raised his eyebrows but said nothing.

"Yeah, so I had to open him up before he was ready. I got him greased up good, then put my fingers in there. But he wanted the whole fist."

A loud groan of protest nearly drowned him out. But he saw Bruno stroking his thigh. There was a lump there. When he realized Gerry was looking at him, he pulled his hand back, revealing a rather long line in his trousers. He blushed and made a 'go on' gesture.

Gerry was surprised the story was interesting for these guys. He didn't pretend to know what went on in the minds of straight guys. He told them about the furry hole, the hands-free orgasm, and blasting his load in the guy's hole.

Lex said, "So, are you guys boyfriends now?"

Gerry laughed. "Fuck, no. I fuck 'em and forget 'em." He raised his hand for a high five. Lex didn't return the gesture, but Hal and Bruno smacked his open palm, symbolizing their approval of Gerry's tale.

Gerry admitted to himself that it felt good being one of the guys. He didn't want to do this all the time, but it was one of the more interesting times he'd had at work. He thought they'd shun him, but they welcomed him in for opening up.

SUBMISSION

Monday night was dead, but he went to the Stud for funk night. The Stud was a fixture on Folsom Street since the 1960s. They'd recently expanded into the defunct church next door called, "The Universal Life Corral." The bar had been packed, and although it was now twice as wide, it was even more packed than before.

The music was good. The dance floor moved in rhythm, hips swaying, arms flying skyward. A few brave women joined the crowd of mustachioed gay men, flirting to no avail. Gerry watched, amused by the whole scene.

Gerry was on his third beer when an older man dressed all in black leather approached him. He wasn't like the queens in the Castro. His Dehner boots looked good with the jodhpurs. He was handsome. He put a hand on Gerry's cheek. "Beautiful man."

Gerry was pretty sure this guy hadn't even looked at his cock. The man was drawn to his face, which was fairly handsome. His nose was big, but his brown eyes glittered and wavy brown hair framed his brow. The leather man was handsome, too. He was furry, tall, with a thick mustache.

Gerry was pretty sure the guy was a top. He said, "Sorry, man, strictly top."

The older gentleman grinned. "How do you know? Have you ever tried it?"

Something about the man's voice made Gerry aroused. There was a subtle dominance. He felt confused.

The leatherman recognized the confusion and took advantage. "If you let me, I'll teach you how good it can feel to get fucked."

The beer had stripped away a layer of inhibition. Gerry had tried a few times, but it hadn't worked. The pain was too much for him. "Dude, it hurts like fuck."

The leather man smiled. "I'm an expert. You won't believe it. Come on, what do you have to lose? I'll stop if you don't like it. But you'll be begging for more."

Gerry liked the fatherly vibe this older man gave off. He made up his mind. "Fuck it, I'm a trisexual. I'll try anything once."

The leather man grinned. "I live next door. You won't have time to change your mind." With that, the leather daddy grabbed him by the wrist and led him to an apartment next to the Stud, on the second floor.

The first thing that struck him was a leather hammock hung from the ceiling. Gerry knew what a sling was. It was designed so a guy could lay back and get fucked easily. The daddy unzipped his pants and pulled out a modest cock. He jerked it, staring at Gerry's face.

"So handsome. Fuck, you're handsome."

Gerry was accustomed to being objectified for his cock, not his face. It was strange. He liked it. This guy hadn't once looked at his crotch. So when Gerry dropped his trousers, the daddy took a step back.

"Holy shit. That's fucking huge. Turn around, I wanna see what you got back there."

Again, Gerry wasn't used to his dick being ignored.

Sure, the daddy acknowledged it, but he didn't fixate on it. Gerry turned around and the leather man whistled.

"Goddamn! I love a soft round ass. I wanna eat that now. Get in the sling."

Gerry obeyed the dominant older man. He hadn't ever fucked a guy in a sling, but he'd seen a couple of 16mm flicks at the Tearoom Theater. He knew he was supposed to put his feet on the chains and scoot his ass forward. His huge cock hung between his legs.

"Move that out of the way."

Gerry threw it over one thigh. He was having second thoughts, but then the man knelt and buried his nose between Gerry's ass cheeks. Nobody had ever done this for him before, and he'd never done it to anyone else. He preferred to just stick his finger in. It was quicker.

Gerry wasn't prepared for the heady sensation. The man's tongue tickled his hole, then invaded it, slicking it up with spit. It felt fantastic. He wanted it to last a long time. He dreaded the feeling of a hard cock in there. He'd never liked it before, why would he like it now?

The leather man brought out a jar filled with a solid white substance. Gerry wondered what it could be.

"Coconut oil. It's solid at room temperature, but it melts at body temperature." The man dug his fingers in and brought out a lump of the solid vegetable fat. It was harder than Crisco. He put it against Gerry's hole and pushed it in with his tongue. He kept eating his ass, pushing the melting fat deeper.

"It tastes a lot better than Crisco." The leather man looked up, his chin greasy. Gerry was in heaven. He took the man by the ears and pulled him back to his hole. The spit and oil felt good. He jumped when the daddy stuck a finger in his hole. It felt weird.

The man put his hand on Gerry's stomach to calm him. "Relax, just let me take care of you."

Gerry had to admit it felt good to lie back and let someone else do the hard work.

The man opened a drawer and held up a strange bottle. It was an enema.

"You need a quick rinse. Trust me, it will feel a lot better."

Gerry was taken aback. But he didn't have a chance to protest. The man put the nozzle in his hole and squeezed. A cool stream filled his rectum. He felt an urge to let it go. The leather man held up a wash basin and caught the stream as it sprayed out of Gerry's ass.

"Oh, you were pretty clean. Good boy."

The man left and emptied the pan. He returned with a dildo. It was short and thin.

"You need a little warm-up. I'll go slow, don't worry."

Gerry felt a sense of dread. Was he ready for this? The man oiled up the fleshy plastic cock. He held the slick dildo against Gerry's hole and gave a gentle nudge. Gerry's ass lips parted slightly, allowing the tip in. Then he felt pressure. The leather daddy stood over him, a bottle of poppers in his hand. He held it under Gerry's nose. A warm rush flooded through him. He felt a jolt of pain, but he was too far in the clouds to protest. Then, there was a long, slippery slide. The dildo was in. It didn't hurt; it felt good. Gerry felt conquered, invaded. He was ashamed how good it felt.

The leather daddy must have been a psychic. "Don't be ashamed. Just let the feeling come." He held the bottle under Gerry's nose again, then handed it to him. "You're in control. Tell me if it's okay."

Gerry nodded.

When the man pulled the dildo back, it felt incredible, like he was taking a shit, but better. The head pressed on his prostate. His cock leaked. When he slid it back in, it didn't feel as good. It felt unnatural to have something move that way in his ass. But it wasn't unpleasant, just different. As the man increased the frequency, it all started to come together. Gerry took a big whiff of the amyl.

When his mind came back into his body, the dildo was flying in and out of his ass completely, at a rapid clip. He couldn't believe how good it felt.

"You like that, don't you."

Gerry said, "Fuck, that feels good."

The man said, "You're ready for the next one." He pulled out a medium-sized dildo. It was about six inches long and maybe four and a half inches around. He slicked it up and pressed it against Gerry's hole. "Ready?"

Gerry took a whiff and smiled. "Go for it."

Another burst of pain, far off in the distance, somewhere down below. Gerry groaned. But this fatter dildo really pressed hard on his prostate gland. He could feel precum dribbling on his thigh. His soft cock began to stiffen. It rose skyward.

The daddy said, "Oh yeah, you like that. Don't you boy?"

Gerry didn't have a father growing up. Being called boy by such a paternal figure was like catnip.

"Yes, sir. I love it."

"You want the real thing?"

Gerry begged. "Yes, sir. I do. Please."

The man smiled. "All in good time. Let me warm you up some more." He moved the dildo back and forth, massaging Gerry's prostate.

Gerry had never seen so much precum come out of his dick. He hardly ever had it. Maybe with a guy as hot as Charlie, but not like this. It was a goopy mess. It ran down his hard shaft, crossed his big balls, and puddled between his legs in the sling.

Gerry didn't need the poppers now. He didn't want to miss a thing. His eyes connected with the father figure hovering over him. He leaned his head back, eyes fluttering, and moaned. The dildo was flying in and out of his ass faster than ever. Every second felt like an hour of pure bliss.

With a loud pop, Mr. Leather pulled out the Dildo and let Gerry's hole throb, hungry for more.

"Yeah, son, you're ready." The leather man unzipped his pants, pulling out a fairly average cock. His pubic hairs were a salt-and-pepper gray. He placed the throbbing head to Gerry's hole and pressed. With very little resistance, the head popped in. Gerry felt a momentary burst of pain. The man pressed forward, filling Gerry's ass. It didn't hurt at all. It felt better than the dildo because it was warm and spongy. And there was an invisible exchange of energy between the two, a connection that Gerry had never felt. Being filled with another man's cock was a subtle submission, a giving away of power. Lying in the sling, legs up, filled with this daddy's cock, Gerry expected to feel shame, but it wasn't there. Giving away control was its own kind of power. He relaxed, nodding.

The leather man took long, slow strokes, his head sliding out of the hole and back in. Gerry could feel his ass close, then reopen as the head came gently forward. Each time, the pace increased slightly. After about twenty strokes, the pace was rapid. Gerry felt a strong wave of pleasure wash over him as endorphins flooded his brain.

"Oh, yeah," the man said, "you're in the sweet spot now."

Gerry knew he was. It felt almost as good as fucking a hole. When the daddy sped up, it felt just as good. He sighed and relaxed more, letting the cock fill his hole. Each time the glans passed his prostate, a little more juice came out of Gerry's huge cock. He held it upright, nearly smacking the daddy in the face, and stroked it with both hands.

"Fuck me, daddy." He wanted it bad.

The man obliged. His hips thrust against Gerry's ass, causing his soft ass cheeks to ripple. Over and over the onslaught continued. Gerry surrendered with each stroke, letting this father figure teach him the joys of passive anal sex.

The leather man leaned over slightly, enough to take the tip of Gerry's cock head between his lips. He licked and slurped, locked onto the meat. It became too much. Gerry felt that building sensation that signaled impending orgasm. He stopped stroking.

"Wait, you're gonna make me come."

The daddy stopped licking and sucking, concentrating on fucking instead. He ground his hips, twisting left, right, straight on, over and over. Gerry's cock was too big and heavy, it teetered to one side. Gerry felt his legs shake. The chains of the sling rattled.

"Oh, yeah," said the leather man, "Daddy's little boy is right there, isn't he?"

"Yes, sir." It was instinct. Gerry knew to call this man sir. It was the only form of address that made sense. He was dominant and Gerry was submissive. It was such a relief. His constant control in sex was more exhausting than he realized. Sitting back and letting Daddy drive.

The building sensation was back. Gerry's cock rose, pulling against gravity until it was straight up and down. A thin stream of precum trickled down the prepuce. The leather daddy licked it up, sending spasms of pleasure down the shaft and across Gerry's body.

It was too late, he was going to come. The leather daddy knew it. He picked up his pace. His breaths grew shallow. His eyes fluttered.

"Oh, shit, I'm gonna come," said the older man.

"Fuck, me too!" Gerry felt the unmistakeable throbbing and his massive balls pulled up tight.

As the first load fired skyward, the older man came inside Gerry. They were in perfect sync. Each blast of cum from Gerry's cock was in time with the warm blasts up his ass. The leather daddy was shiny with sweat, his leather pants glistening in the dim light of the apartment. His breaths grew heavy, and he let out a long, loud grunt of pleasure.

"Damn, son! You're a natural! Was that really your first time?"

Gerry felt self-conscious for the first time. He pulled away from the daddy, letting the soft cop flop out of his throbbing asshole.

"Uh, yeah. Look, I gotta go." Gerry struggled to get out of the sling. The daddy grabbed his arm and helped hoist him to his feet.

The cold afterglow was mutual. The man stuffed his cock back in his leather pants and zipped up.

"Sorry your first time was with me. I don't do repeats."

Gerry smiled. "Neither do I."

❧ 4 ❧

BROKEN PUMP

The next day at work, Gerry felt sore. He walked with a slight limp, which Bruno noticed.

"Hey Gerry Fairy? Did you injure your dick fucking some boy last night?"

Gerry grinned and nodded. He didn't want anyone to know how much he liked getting fucked the night before.

"We're going back to the Dog for lunch. Why don't you come with us and tell us a new story? They're kinda hot. I ain't no fag, but you still get me hard."

Gerry was flummoxed. He thought straight was straight and gay was gay. Why would Bruno want to hear about his exploits? Worse, why did he want to know today of all days, when the real story was embarrassing?

Hal rounded the corner, checking his gas stick. "What's that? Another Gerry Fairy story? Fuckin' A."

Gerry couldn't stand it. "Why the fuck do you want to hear about some faggot sex? Unless you're queer..."

Bruno's face contorted into a snarl. "You're so fucking uppity, Gerry. We try to be friendly and you give us attitude. Your stories are good. Why do you care if we want to hear them? You should be flattered."

"Well I'm not."

Hal patted Bruno on the shoulder. "Leave him be. It's different for fags. Have a little respect."

Gerry turned red. "Fine, I got a story that will freak your shit out. Wait until lunch. You might choke, so be prepared."

Out of the corner of his eye, he saw Lex fold his arms and shake his head, a mischievous grin hiding under his mustache.

Over chili dogs and Coke, Gerry began recounting the unusual turn of events at the Stud.

Hal said, "Was that your first time getting fucked?"

Gerry nodded and continued. "If you relax, it feels just like the best part of taking a shit."

Expecting laughter, he was surprised when all three men sat quietly, sipping their Coke and eating the wretched hot dogs.

Lex spoke up. "You know that's kind of weird, right?"

Bruno leapt to Gerry's defense. "Nah, man, I totally get it. My girlfriend stuck a finger up my ass once, and it felt fucking great. I shot a huge load."

Lex smiled. "I stand corrected."

Gerry looked at Bruno with a sly grin. "Has she ever let you do it in the butt?"

Bruno said, "No way man. I ain't as big as you, but I'm pretty damn big. She said she wouldn't let me so much as put a finger in her." He held up his hand, with its long, fat fingers, and played an imaginary piano in the air.

Hal chuckled and buried his short fingers in his jacket pockets. Gerry thought he might have detected a little flush in his cheeks.

Bruno said, "Besides, we broke up a couple of weeks ago. I was gonna tell you about it, but it still kinda hurts."

The table grew quiet again.

Bruno asked, "You didn't say how big he was. Was he big?"

Gerry shrugged. "On the smaller side of average. Like a little over five inches, maybe. And not very thick."

Bruno blurted out, "Oh well."

The other three men exchanged glances that asked, "What does that mean?"

Lex said it outright. "You thinking about trying it out on someone?"

The table erupted in laughter. Bruno reddened. "Maybe. Maybe I'd fuck a girl in the ass, hell even a guy if they were loose enough to take me." To emphasize this, he grabbed his cock through his jeans. It was plenty long and thick.

Lex said, "Yeah, Bruno, we know about your dick. We've all seen it."

Hal said, "Don't drop the soap around this guy."

Bruno clenched his fists, then relaxed, laughing at himself. "Did I just say that?"

More laughter.

Back at the plant, a siren went off. It was Lift Pump number one. Too many rag balls (plastic and rubber) had built up, and the pump stopped working. There were silos that could hold the flow buildup, but they had about three hours before they overflowed, causing a spill.

Lift pump repair was a three-man job. Gerry was a lab technician, but this case was all hands on deck. The repair guy was at the Eastside plant. He had to rush over through traffic, and it was going to be close, so the three men had to start the job without him. It was going to be a shitty afternoon.

Gerry suited up in waders and joined Bruno and Hal. Hal turned the crank wheel that opened the door to the pump. A steady flow of murky water leaked out. Bruno was the most qualified to operate the crane that removed the pump for repair, so he was up top. It was just Hal and Gerry. After a while, the solid debris began to flow out. That was the shit. The room began to smell. Hal's gas stick went off.

"Shit, Gerry, the hydrogen sulfide is at five. We gotta clear out and let this shit subside."

Gerry was relieved to breathe fresh air. His lungs had started to burn, so he knew the gas buildup was serious. After about fifteen minutes, it dropped below one, and they were able to get back to work. By then, the pump lift chamber was mostly just heaps of inorganic waste, or 'rag balls' as Bruno called them. Condoms, plastic bags, tampon applicators, and all kinds of other non-flushable crud had jammed the gears.

Gerry heard the chamber door creak. It would be Kit, the old man who had been repairing lift pumps for decades. But when Gerry turned, he got a surprise. It was a massive man in his thirties. He barely fit in his hip waders. Bulging muscles mushroomed out of the top of the rubber overalls.

Gerry said, "Where's Kit?"

The muscular hunk grinned. "I'm Norm. Kit retired last month. Didn't you go to the party?"

Hal broke in. "We weren't invited."

Gerry couldn't help but stare at the blond Adonis. His pale blue eyes had heavy lids that made him look like someone who had just woken up from a nap.

Hal said, "Gerry, you're good. Go take a shower. We got some Lava soap in the cabinet. That should take out most of the smell."

Gerry wanted to stay and eat Norm alive with his eyes, but he wanted to get the stink off much more. He hosed off his waders at the top of the stairs and hung them to dry. They'd need to go through the disinfecting wash before he could wear them again.

Gerry stepped into the hot shower, sliding the caustic soap across his body until it lathered. It didn't burn, but it felt like it was taking off the top layer of skin. Lava wasn't your mother's lavender-scented olive oil soap. It was hardcore. He got lost in thought as he rinsed the lather from his body, enjoying the clean smell. While he was in there, he figured he'd wash every inch of his skin. It took a long time. He paid close attention to the crevices and between his toes. He switched to Ivory for his dick and ass. That was when the guys walked in. He supposed with a massive guy like Norm, the job had taken half the time.

Gerry said, "That was quick."

Norm stopped in his tracks. "Holy fuck."

Gerry groaned a little. He prepared for the onslaught of stupid questions.

"Is that real?"

Gerry shook his head. "It's not." It was his favorite response to an idiotic question that every guy, gay or straight, would ask him in the showers.

Norm cracked a smile as he stripped off his shirt, revealing a Lou Ferrigno upper body. Massive, with tits like earplugs on a salad plate. Next came the pants. They were the baggy kind that bodybuilders wear, but with Norm's quads, they were pretty tight. A plump, half-hard, football-shaped cock bounced against his legs. The head was small, and it grew fat in the middle. The base was narrow. As he turned to hang his pants on the hook, he revealed his creamy white ass. It was the kind of ass that knocked drinks off of tables. In fact, you could probably set down a beer bottle on it and it wouldn't fall off.

It was Gerry's turn to ask a dumb question. "Were you born with that ass or did you build it yourself?"

Norm said, "I bought it at Macy's." Touché.

Gerry's cock had a mind of its own. He was at work. He was at work. He was at work. No! Fuck! Norm was so hot, he was getting a boner. He was hung, a grower and a show-er. His cock lengthened, still soft, but reaching for his knees. He didn't have any way to hide his arousal.

Norm raised an eyebrow. "Fuck, that's big. Lucky guy. You must get a lot of tail."

Bruno butted into the conversation. "He has to search pretty hard to find a guy…I mean someone who could take it."

Now it was Norm who couldn't hide his arousal. His fat cock lifted off his leg.

Hal had his furry back turned to the other guys.

Bruno watched, fascinated, while Norm and Gerry's erections blossomed.

He said, "Shit. This is embarrassing." Gerry broke his blatant gaze from Norm's plump cock and gasped. Bruno was rock-hard. His cock was at least eight inches long and six inches around. It throbbed in the air like a baby's arm waving an apple.

Norm started it. He put a hand on his cock and gave it a few tugs. Bruno didn't hesitate. He started to jerk off, stroking the huge meat. Gerry shrugged and did his best to jack off with them. He had to lift it close to his chest and use both hands.

Bruno said, "Holy mother of god. I never seen it hard. You're a goddamn freak." He caught himself when he saw Gerry's face form a scowl. "I mean, it's freaking hot as fuck."

Hal was busy soaping himself off, but he stole a glance over his shoulder and jumped. Without thinking, he whirled around to join in the circle jerk. He had his little furry cock between his thumb and forefinger. Next to Gerry, they looked like two different species. He wasn't a grower or a show-er.

Then, to Gerry's astonishment, Hal knelt down in front of Bruno, taking his huge head into his mouth.

Bruno said, "That's right, little buddy. Just like that. Just like I taught you."

Hal slurped up Bruno's head, bobbing deeper and

deeper until it pushed into his throat, showing a lump. Gerry's head swam. Had this been going on right under his nose? Watching one macho straight man sucking off another was a major turn-on.

Norm reached out and stroked Gerry's cock with one hand and himself with the other. Three hands were better than two. Gerry couldn't help himself. He bent his head slightly, putting one of Norm's massive nipples in his mouth. The guy was a giant, maybe 6'4" inches and wide as a truck. The nipple hardened, and Norm let out a shaky sigh.

"Yeah, suck my tits."

Bruno sidestepped, and Hal crawled on his knees. Bruno put a free hand on Gerry's cock. Four hands were perfect. Bruno put his free hand on the back of Hal's head and pushed into him, causing the little teddy bear to choke and gag. Hal didn't seem to care. He kept going, gagging on Bruno's big monster, stroking the base with both hands.

Bruno's breath grew shallow. "Oh shit, dude, I'm gonna come. Let me do it in your mouth this time."

Hal nodded as best he could with his throat full of cock. Bruno pulled on Hal's head repeatedly, fucking his skull. His breaths grew faster.

"Oh shit! Oh fuck, Hal. I'm coming." Bruno bucked his hips.

"Mmmph!" Hal pulled off Bruno, gasping as the huge cock shot all over his face and open mouth.

Hal gave a few rapid tugs on his tiny pecker and it sprayed the shower floor.

Gerry felt a warm splash on his leg. Norm had shot his load. All the cum had pushed Gerry past that point that every man knows. He didn't even mind the three men watching him, slack-jawed in amazement. It turned him on more, forcing him towards orgasm. Hal cupped Gerry's balls and licked them, sending him over the edge. Gerry's balls lifted off of Hal's hand.

"Oh, shit. I'm coming!"

Bruno shouted, "Fucking A! Do it!"

Gerry's cock erupted, shooting sperm skyward as though he hadn't come for two weeks. It rained down on all four men.

Hal said, "Fuck that's beautiful."

Bruno said, "Oh, you don't know how long I've wanted to see that." One by one, the hands fell away until Gerry was left to squeeze out the last few droplets on his own.

A LIFT HOME

As if nothing had happened, the men returned to soaping up and rinsing off, mostly to get the cum out of their hair and off their skin. In the silence, Gerry felt his head spinning. He thought queer was queer and straight was straight. Apparently, he had been wrong. He felt something brush his leg. Norm was hard again. His pretty pink cock throbbed against Gerry's leg. Gerry rubbed his washboard stomach and smiled.

Norm said quietly, "When can I see you again?"

Gerry was about to pull his cold shoulder routine, but he didn't. Instead, he said, "I can't ride MUNI in my clothes. Can I maybe get a ride home from you?"

Norm slapped Gerry's ass. "Only if you put out."

Two days earlier, Gerry would have been taken aback. But looking down at Norm's fat six-inch cock, he felt his butthole twitch. He'd been fucked and he wanted it again. It wasn't like him.

Without thinking, he said, "Okay, but I don't suck cock."

Norm whispered in his ear, "That's okay. I don't either."

When Gerry returned to the lab, Lex smiled. "What

were you guys doing in the shower? I thought I heard someone scream."

Gerry shrugged as he picked up his water testing kit. "The water got cold for a minute." He didn't know if there was a code of silence, but it seemed better to play it safe. Lex wasn't part of the club yet.

Then, to Gerry's astonishment, Lex said, "Huh. It sounded to me like Hal was blowing Bruno again."

Gerry dropped his kit, shattering a test tube. "Shit!"

Lex laughed. "You didn't know, did you? That's why Bruno broke up with his girlfriend. She saw teeth marks on his cock."

Still waters run deep. Lex was full of surprises.

Gerry said, "Uh, no, I didn't."

Lex shrugged. "Was it weird doing it with Kit in there? He's a little creepy for an old guy."

Gerry said, "It was this new guy, Norm. Built like a brick shithouse."

A hint of a frown crossed Lex's face. "Oh."

Gerry cleaned up the test tube shards and replaced it with another. He had to test twice before the water was ready to release. The backup and muck-stirring from the lift pump had created a higher-than-normal level of bacteria.

He and Lex wrapped up at the same time. As they walked out together, they nearly crashed into Norm, who came bounding forward.

"Hey, I'm Norm." He reached out a hand.

"Lex." Lex ended the shake early. He kept walking, waving goodbye without turning around, like Liza Minelli in the last scene of Cabaret. Norm and Gerry were alone.

"Your place or mine?" Norm put his strong hand on Gerry's ass and caressed it. "Oh, shit, that's a sweet little ass. I can't wait to fuck it."

Gerry nearly melted. He said, "Let's go to mine."

It was so strange. That leather man had turned him into a greedy, cock-hungry pig. He felt that incredible relaxing vibe. He didn't have to do all the work. He could let someone else do the driving, so to speak. He thought he'd feel ashamed to be a bottom, but he felt proud. His cock had been in such demand. Nobody had even noticed his ass until the day before. He hoped Norm would flip and let him fuck that beautiful white ass, too. He felt a swelling in his khakis and quickly thought about the ocean in an attempt to make the swelling go down. It worked.

❦ 6 ❦

CRYSTAL AND BEER

Norm was a good driver. Gerry was relieved. He'd been in the car with some bodybuilders who let the steroids get the better of them. They drove like maniacs. Not Norm.

Norm wound his way over Twin Peaks and gently glided into the Castro, searching for parking. They ended up parking two blocks away. It was San Francisco. They climbed the hill to Gerry's place, barely able to keep their hands off each other.

Upstairs, Gerry cracked a couple of beers. Norm pulled out a baggie full of powder.

"You do speed?"

Gerry was taken aback. "Uh, no."

Norm had already tipped the bag on the coffee table, cutting the crystals with a credit card and lining them up in four neat rows. "There's a first time for everything."

"I gotta work tomorrow."

Norm said, "Call in sick," as he rolled a twenty-dollar bill into a tube. He leaned forward. "This is how you do it." He snorted a line in each nostril, then held out the twenty to Gerry.

"Trust me, you're gonna love it."

Gerry shook his head.

”Don't be a pussy.” He put the twenty in Gerry's hand.

Gerry had smoked grass. He didn't like it much. Speed was way out of his comfort zone. But things were changing all around him. He didn't know which way was up anymore.

”Fuck it.” He picked up the twenty and snorted the short line. It burned.

”Quick, do the other.”

He obeyed the massive bodybuilder. His eyes watered as the bitter drug struck his sinuses. Then, about ten seconds later, the world became the best place on earth. He felt his cock harden. He looked at Norm, who was already kicking off his clothes.

”Oh shit. This feels fuckin' great.”

Norm grabbed his fat football cock and waved it in the air. “You can fuck all night on speed. Your ass is going to be so sore.”

Gerry said, “Yours too.”

Norm shook his head. “Nope. Not me. The last thing that went in my ass got chopped off.”

Those words were ominous, but Gerry was too high to care. Norm picked him up like an infant and carried him to the bed. He threw Gerry down and unbuckled his belt. Gerry's cock was rock hard, trapped in his pants. Norm couldn't help him. While Gerry struggled to escape his pants, Norm pulled off his shirt, tearing it with his big brutal hands. At last, the two were naked, hearts pounding in their chest with artificial excitement.

Norm knelt on the floor, pulling Gerry's ass to his mouth. He sucked and spat, his tongue invading Gerry's hole. He felt an emergency coming on.

”I gotta—“

Norm waved him. “Yep. That's the speed. Go.”

Gerry emptied himself out. He took the hand-held

shower and stepped into the tub, washing himself up there. He wanted to be clean for his top.

After Gerry toweled off, he found Norm, who had already discovered the tub of Crisco in the drawer of the bedside table. He had spread it on his cock, which shined in the bright lights of the bedroom. Gerry turned off the overhead, so only the bedside lamp lit the room.

"Come over here." Gerry was short enough that his cock went straight between Norm's legs as he hugged him to his hips. This giant towered over him. Again, Norm picked Gerry up, but this time, he lowered him onto his hard cock.

Gerry braced for pain, but it went right in, stretching his hole. The speed had done something. His ass was a pussy. It tingled and throbbed as Norm penetrated him. The bodybuilder carried him around the apartment, setting him down on the dresser, the bed, the arm of the couch, and the kitchen counter. He fucked and fucked. Gerry's cock lay against Norm's chest, the head brushing the fat nipples. Gerry leaned forward, pressing his cock into Norm, and sucking his nipples while he licked his own head. He felt like coming, but it just stayed there, on the edge, a nonstop bliss. It was like a roller coaster caught at the top of the hill.

Gerry's ass was stretched further than it had ever been. As Norm slid in and out, the fat football stretched and released. It rubbed against his prostate. He soon tasted the salty precum as it dripped on Norm's nipple. The room was spinning.

"Oh god, Norm, I love you!" It felt true in the moment, but as soon as he said it, Norm's countenance grew dark.

"That's the speed talking. Shut up and let me fuck you."

Norm laid Gerry on his back in missionary. As he

fucked him, his heavy body pressed against Gerry's cock, massaging it with his washboard abs and giant pecs.

Again, that feeling of wanting to come washed over Gerry. It built like a sneeze that never quite happened. Except instead of a sneeze, it was an orgasm. And being so close felt incredible.

Norm rolled Gerry onto his stomach and fucked him from behind. With his cock pressed into the bed, his orgasmic eternity shifted back into his ass. He felt, he thought, how a woman must feel. The orgasm in his ass was endless. He began to contract involuntarily.

"Yeah, that's it. Squeeze my cock with your pussy."

Gerry didn't have a choice but to obey. The anal orgasm built until it reached a crescendo but never stopped. It just stayed level, turned up to the maximum. Waves rippled through his lower body.

Norm rolled Gerry onto his side and held one leg aloft. From this angle, he was able to go deep enough to hit the back of the rectum. This pressed on Gerry's bladder, making him aware of the beer he'd drunk earlier.

"Norm, I need to piss."

"Do it in my mouth."

He pulled out of Gerry's ass and clamped his mouth over the massive cock head. Gerry didn't have time to care, it was too urgent. Another first: he pissed in Norm's mouth, who greedily swallowed it up. Even pissing felt like bliss. He shivered with delight, all his senses sending a current of ecstasy through his body.

Gerry sat astride Norm, facing the giant as he bounced on his lap, the cock sliding back and forth inside him. Norm put his mouth on the head of the cock, slurping, licking, and sucking.

Gerry said, "Fuck, that feels good."

Norm stopped. "Don't get used to it." But he returned to giving head, what little he could. Gerry bounced like a cowboy on a horse. Norm's cock was the perfect length. It never slipped out, and in most positions, it didn't punch into the back wall. Gerry wanted to eat Norm's ass and fuck him, but that wasn't in the cards, or so he thought.

Suddenly, Norm lifted Gerry off of him and stood him on his feet. Gerry swayed, overcome with the overwhelming joy and pleasure that the drug and fucking had caused. Then, to his delight, Norm got on his knees on the bed, displaying his perfect beautiful ass with its tight pink hole.

"Eat my ass."

Gerry hesitated. "Don't cut my tongue off."

"Shut up and eat me out."

Gerry was an expert at eating ass. He'd loosened up hundreds of guys this way. He expertly licked and tongued Norm's hole. The huge bodybuilder wriggled, squealing like a girl.

"Shit, that feels good."

Gerry said, "I can make you feel so good you won't know what hit you."

Norm spread the muscular white cheeks of his ass apart, allowing Gerry to dig deeper in the hole with his tongue. He could tell Norm was not a bottom. It was just too tight. As much as he wanted to fuck the guy, he knew it wouldn't work. Length didn't matter much, but Gerry was bigger than a beer can in girth. No first-timer, no matter how badly they wanted it, could ever take him. He'd have to content himself with sticking a finger or two in the tight hole. He didn't really want to, in fact. He wanted to lay back and let Norm do all the fucking.

With his face buried between the two globes of butt flesh, Gerry reached under and took Norm's fat cock in one hand, jerking it like a farmer milking a goat. Norm bucked with pleasure.

"Oh god. Fuck me, Gerry. I want it."

Gerry knew better, but Norm insisted. The body-builder spent five minutes greasing up Gerry's cock, shoving some Crisco up his own ass. He stood over the colossal tower of cock and sat. It was like sitting on a barstool. Gerry felt his cock buckle at the base from the pressure of this 275-pound hunk of muscle sitting on him. The head barely entered him.

"Oh, fuck! That feels so good!"

It might have felt good for Norm, but not for Gerry. His cock hurt. He cupped two hands under Norm's ass, trying with all his might to lift the bodybuilder off of him.

"Please, Norm, you're hurting me."

Norm stood, jumped down off the bed, and lifted Gerry like he was a rag doll, facing away from him, planted him on his fat cock, and then let him fall forward. He walked Gerry around the house like a wheelbarrow, fucking him hard to move him in the direction he desired.

Gerry would have felt humiliated, but the speed was too powerful to allow shame or guilt. Everything he did with Norm was pleasure, save perhaps for the near cock-breaking experience of serving as Norm's barstool. His arms grew tired. Norm held him by the waist, lifting him to his feet. They fucked, standing up, Gerry's cock swinging to and fro to the rhythm of Norm's fucking.

The phone rang; Gerry ignored it until he looked out the curtains and saw daylight. His answering machine kicked in. It was Bruno.

"Hey, dude. Where are you? The boss is looking for you. Give us a callback. I hope yesterday wasn't too weird for you."

Frantically, Gerry broke away and called in sick. Norm stood by him, cramming his dick up his butthole while he tried to explain why he hadn't called sooner.

When the call was over, the two men retired to the

bedroom. Norm said he was tired. His fat pink dick looked red now. Gerry wondered if his ass looked the same. They'd fucked like rabbits all night. Nobody came. Norm lay on the bed and crashed, leaving Gerry wide awake and alone. Norm probably had more tolerance for the speed. Gerry's mind raced about, skipping from thought train to thought train, never connecting. The light in the room changed as the afternoon sun filtered in through his west-facing windows. It grew dark. At last, he fell into a sound sleep, waking in the morning to find Norm gone.

HAPPY ENDING

Gerry limped to the shower and washed off the grease, stink, and sweat from his night of passion and day of sleeplessness. He wasn't hungry, but he forced down some toast and caught the MUNI to the treatment plant. It hurt every time the streetcar went over a bump.

He did his best to walk normal past the guys into the lab. Bruno shouted, "You look sick. Go home! Don't get us all sick, too."

Gerry smiled and waved. He ran to the toilet and threw up the toast. He made himself a cup of weak tea and ate a stale donut. It settled his stomach a little.

Lex brightened when Gerry walked in. "Hey, we missed you yesterday. Are you alright?" Lex saw his coworker struggling to sit down on the lab stool and said, "Was that Norm?"

Gerry shook his head, waited, then nodded.

"What did he do to you? You look like death."

Gerry said, "We overdid it. He had some speed. I never tried it before."

Lex said, "That shit's deadly. Why the hell did you do it?"

Gerry said, "If it's any comfort, I don't think I ever want to do it again." His ass was burning. He shifted from cheek to cheek, then stood. He felt sick again but managed to keep it down.

Lex did something very out of character. He walked over, put his hands on Gerry's shoulders, and gave him a gentle massage. It was exactly the medicine Gerry needed.

"God, Lex, that feels good. Your wife is so lucky."

Lex stiffened.

Gerry said, "I hit a nerve, didn't I?"

Lex sighed, the breath rushing past Gerry's cheek. "She died two years ago."

Gerry swiveled around to face his coworker. He understood in that moment why Lex was so reserved, so quiet.

"Oh, buddy, I didn't know."

Lex said, "Nobody knows. Well, you do now."

Gerry instinctively wrapped his arms around his friend and pulled him close. This time, Lex's sigh was more one of exasperation.

"It's been two years. I don't need a hug."

Gerry let go. "I didn't know. I mean, shit, you should have said something."

Lex shook his head. "Why?"

It was Gerry's turn to give an exasperated sigh. "Dude, you're my best friend. You know you could have trusted me not to say anything if you didn't want me to. I got your back."

Lex stared at Gerry. "I'm your best friend?" The men broke the ensuing silence with gales of laughter.

Gerry said, "Come to think of it, you are. I can't think of anyone closer."

Lex said, "Well, shit, that means you're my best friend too. Ain't that beautiful?" He turned back to his work, missing the odd look that came over Gerry's face.

As the day wore on, Gerry began to feel better. He hadn't brought lunch. It was hard to tolerate the foul odor at the plant, and he didn't want to so much as breathe the air near a chili dog, so he begged off and stayed behind with Les. Together they walked to a quiet cafe near the State University and had bowls of chicken soup with French bread. It settled Gerry's stomach some more.

On the walk back, Lex asked a few questions. The first was, "When did you find out you were gay?"

Gerry shrugged. "I think around puberty. I lost interest in girls right when the guys were starting to sniff around them. I just wanted the guys to sniff around me."

"Was that when you got, uh, big down there?"

Gerry wrinkled his nose but smiled. "Yeah, I mean, I was always big, but the year I turned gay I went from big to enormous. And it kept going until senior year of High School."

"Did the other guys tease you?"

Gerry said, "What do you think? Hell yes. They'd stomp and whinny like a horse when I walked by. The girls were all over me but they didn't want this when they saw it. It wasn't until I moved into the city that I finally found some loose fags to fuck."

Lex said, "Fag is an ugly word. Why do you use it?"

Gerry shrugged. "It's okay when a gay guy says it. It's like queer or queen. It's our word when we say it. Geez, Lex, you are just full of questions today."

Lex tossed his dirty blond hair and chuckled. "I know, sorry. I've been doing a lot of thinking."

"About what?"

A thin bead of sweat ran down Lex's forehead. "I guess I've been thinking about men. I don't want to be gay, but I might be."

Gerry hugged Lex. "Holy shit, dude, that's fucking awesome! Yes! Please be gay. We'd love to have a hotty like you."

Lex pulled away, briefly, and stopped in his tracks. "I thought I wasn't cool enough to be gay, not like you.

Gerry, you're so confident. And slutty. I mean you're never with the same guy twice."

Gerry's eyes lit up with the compliment. "Yeah, I got a one-night stand mentality. It's not the only way to be gay."

Lex closed his eyes and blurted it out. "I want a guy like you, but you don't want a relationship."

"A guy like me?"

"Okay, I want you, Gerry. God, I hope I didn't just wreck a friendship!"

Gerry said, "Calm down. It's cool. Really."

Lex shook visibly. Gerry held him while he wept. He lifted Lex's chin.

"Hey, buddy, it's gonna be okay. Really."

Lex wiped his nose with his shirt sleeve. "Sorry, I don't know why I'm losing it. I don't get why I feel like this."

Gerry said, "None of us know why we're gay or straight."

Lex added, "Or bi."

"Right. I don't get that, but yeah."

They walked the last three blocks in silence. Gerry felt a strange new emotion towards his coworker. It was like a mixture of fear, arousal, and something unfamiliar but pleasant. What was he afraid of? He'd fucked around at work just a few days before. But then he felt that weird attachment to Norm. And then Norm kicked him to the curb, just like Gerry had done hundreds of times. The only difference was that Gerry let a guy stick a dick in his ass. It was like his ass unclenched and let in not just a cock, but feelings. New feelings. Frightening feelings.

Gerry tried to shut the door on his emotions, but, like the crank wheel that opened the pump door, he couldn't close it once the sludge began to flow. His eyes stung as they climbed the steps to the office.

Gerry said, "Lex, I gotta go to the can. Will you be

alright?" Even as he said the words, his voice began to shake. He felt naked, raw, and vulnerable.

Lex nodded.

Gerry rushed to the stall and locked the door. He unwound a handful of toilet paper, wiping his running nose while the tears came. He heaved, shaking uncontrollably.

"What the fuck?" He thought to himself. *"I've never felt anything like this."*

A knock on the stall door. "Hey, dude, what's going on?" It was Bruno. The last person Gerry wanted to talk to.

"Allergies! Fuck off!" Gerry prayed that his nosy co-worker would let it go. He did.

"Alright, man. Just hurry up; I gotta take a shit."

After about ten minutes, the tears dried up. He washed his face and surrendered the bathroom to Bruno.

Gerry came back to the lab where Lex sat staring at him like an entomologist who'd discovered a new bug.

"Did you catch some feelings there, Ger?"

Gerry nodded. "I don't know what the fuck that was."

Lex put a hand on Gerry's muscular forearm. "Don't think about it; just let it out if you need to."

Gerry wiped his nose with his sleeve. "Nah, I'm alright, really. I just felt really weird."

Lex sat down backward in his chair, leaning over the back, and looked Gerry square in the eye. "You've been in love before, though, haven't you?"

Gerry shook his head. "I don't know what love is."

Lex said, "I do. I know what it looks like coming and going. I loved Maggie. Before I asked her out the first time, it felt like I swallowed a duck. My stomach was in knots, and my heart pounded in my chest. I would break into a sweat every time she looked my way."

Gerry shrugged. "Yeah, I don't know—"

Lex jumped out of the chair and planted his lips on Gerry's. Gerry stumbled backward, but Lex held him firm. Gerry closed his eyes and kissed his coworker back. It felt good.

Lex broke away and said, "Let's take the afternoon off. This shit can wait."

GERRY UNLOCKED HIS DOOR, LETTING LEX LEAD THE way up the stairs to his flat. They cracked a couple of beers and sat on the couch. Gerry felt fear like he'd never known since he first realized he was gay. This was different. He'd let himself be hurt and knew how he must have made so many men feel. He didn't want to hurt Lex. His cock was doing all the thinking, though. He felt it pulsing against his thigh.

Lex put a hand on Gerry's thigh, massaging the big piece of meat through his pant leg. He leaned in for a kiss. Gerry instinctively pulled away. Lex was unphased. He kept leaning in until Gerry returned the kiss. It was strange how good it felt. They kissed for a while, just letting the energy flow between them, breathing each other's air.

When Gerry withdrew, Lex said, "I'm not sure how this will work. We both have the same problem."

Gerry said, "What's that?"

Lex stood, unbuttoned his shirt, and took it off, revealing a surprisingly toned upper body underneath. Then he unbuttoned his loose-fitting pants. As he slowly pulled them down, Gerry could tell he had no underwear. Little by little, Lex tugged his pants down, revealing more and more cock with each inch. Gerry gasped. He hadn't ever seen what Lex was packing. Lex's pants slid past his hips, down his thigh, revealing the endless length of his shaft. Finally, when he was close to his knees, the cock popped out in full glory. It wasn't as thick as Gerry's, but it was as long, perhaps longer.

"Oh, fuck! And you're a virgin." Gerry whined. "I don't think I can take you, and there's no way you could take me."

Lex winked. "I practiced." He turned around, revealing that his ass was stuffed with an extra-large buttplug. "I'm a virgin, yeah, but I'm prepared." He tugged on the end of the plug while pushing out. The massive rubber toy came out, revealing a cavernous hole slick with Crisco.

Gerry's cock was trapped in his tight jeans. He struggled until it broke free, leaping skyward. Lex hovered over Gerry's cock, taking it in his hand. "I can't suck it, but I think I can take it." He slowly sat down, letting the head slip past his sphincter with the skill of a much more experienced man. He sat until the cock filled his rectum.

"Holy shit, Gerry. You're hard as a rock."

Gerry held Lex by his buttocks and gently tilted him until the head of his cock rested against the second hole. He relaxed, letting Lex lower himself further.

Lex said, "The second hole! Oh man, that feels good. I read about it, but I didn't know how good it felt. Mmm!" He bounced up and down, letting the cock slide up into his guts with each downward motion.

Gerry's cock grew longer and thicker inside Lex. He was more turned on than he could remember. As the head slipped in and out of Lex's colon, Gerry shuddered with pleasure.

"Fuck, Lex, keep doing that."

Lex obliged, stroking Gerry's cock head with his insides. Gerry closed his eyes, letting the intense pleasure wash over him. As Lex bounced, his huge cock slapped against Gerry's open thighs. First one, then the other. He felt his pubes tickling Lex's ass. In a few more bounces, Lex sat squarely in Gerry's lap, filled completely with the massive cock. Gerry groaned.

"I never felt like this. I want you so bad."

Lex couldn't hide his discomfort. Between clenched teeth, he said, "I want you, too. Let's try it on the bed."

Lex stood, letting Gerry's cock slide down. When his knees fully straightened, Gerry's cock head left his hole, throbbing in the air, hungry for more ass.

Lex led Gerry by the cock into the bedroom. He lay on his back, his knees tucked to his ears. Lex's impressive cock lay across his chest.

Gerry stood over his coworker. Holding his cock with both hands, he guided it back into Lex's hole. Now it was his turn to let gravity do the work. Lex wriggled, his face screwed up in a grimace. Gerry pulled back.

Lex grabbed Gerry's thigh. "No, keep going. I'm getting used to it."

Gerry pushed forward again until Lex's foot pressed against his thigh. It was an involuntary reaction. Gerry had seen it a hundred times. With his new-found emotions, the foot felt like a rejection. Gerry struggled to hide his shame. He wanted to keep going. To his surprise, Lex let his foot slide past Gerry's thigh, hooking it and pulling. He wanted Gerry to go deeper.

Once he navigated the second hole, he was in the home stretch. Inch after inch vanished inside Lex until Gerry's hips rested firmly against the butt cheeks. Lex pulled his ass open to let Gerry go further. Then he rested, feeling Lex's ass pulsing against his huge cock.

"May I?"

Lex bit his lip, nodding vigorously.

Gerry pulled back slowly, then pushed it home again. Lex's flat belly bulged, revealing the outline of Gerry's cock inside his guts. Gerry had seen it plenty of times, but with Lex, he felt a brand new fascination. It was as if he saw it for the first time. Lex put his hands on his belly, stroking Gerry's cock through the layers of flesh.

"Nnngh! Fuck me harder."

Gerry felt a gush of precum leak out at the words. It slicked up the greasy trail even more, making a slippery trail for him to follow. In short thrusts and jabs, he fucked his friend deep. Lex thrashed from side to side, grunting.

"It's okay, yeah?"

"More." Lex could barely manage to speak a single word.

Gerry took longer strokes. Lex crossed his ankles to pull Gerry towards him. Each time Gerry pulled out, Lex pulled in an ever-increasing pace. He wanted Gerry to cut loose and really fuck him.

"Can I?"

Lex's eyes were all whites. He was incapable of responding. After a long groan and a sigh, Lex nodded his head. "Do it."

Gerry's thrusts grew in length and speed. He popped in and out of Lex's colon, accelerating like a train leaving the station. Soon his hips were a blur. Lex came in and out of consciousness, a massive smile spreading across his face.

In a waking moment, Lex looked into Gerry's eyes and said, "I love you, man."

Suddenly, Gerry understood why Cupid always held a bow and arrow in the paintings. Lex's words pierced his frozen heart, releasing a flood of emotions that could only be love. It pushed Gerry over the edge.

"Oh shit, Lex, I'm gonna come."

Lex said, "Do it."

Gerry took twenty long, fast strokes, then held still, buried all the way inside his friend. His huge heavy balls pulsed as the floodgates opened. He came hard. Lex held his belly, milking Gerry's cock with vigorous strokes. It made Gerry come more. It was the best orgasm of his life. He stayed buried deep, panting, and then he kissed Lex.

The kiss made him collapse on top of him. He felt Lex's monster dong pulsing between them. His friend hadn't come yet. He felt bad. It was too big for him to suck, so he held the head to his lips and used his tongue.

Lex said, "Wait. I want to fuck you next."

Gerry's asshole clenched. Could he take this guy who was so much bigger than Norm? He prepared to shake his head, but it nodded. His heart was stronger than his head. He knew with every fiber of his being that it would be painful, but he wanted to lie back and let Lex have him completely. He wanted the closeness. It was mind-boggling.

In a smooth, skillful motion, Gerry withdrew from Lex. He cupped his hand, expecting a trickle of cum. To his astonishment, the jism poured out like a waterfall, spilling onto the floor and bedspread. Lex's hole gaped and closed in rhythm with his heartbeat. Lex held Gerry's cupped hand to his lips and swallowed what he could.

Gerry went to the bathroom and washed his semen down the sink. When he got back to the bed, Lex had found his can of Crisco. Gerry stood with his butt pointed at Lex's face. Lex lovingly scooped two fingers into the tub and slid them up Gerry's tight hole. He spread the apart, stretching the hole until it loosened up.

"Hand me the poppers." Gerry took the bottle and huffed a big whiff. His ass loosened. Lex had three, then four fingers inside now. It felt good. He was ready.

With another huge huff of poppers, Gerry squatted over Lex's towering cock and guided the head to the opening of his ass. The cheeks were greasy with Crisco. He tried to fit the head inside, but it was flared, like a mushroom, and he couldn't get past.

Lex said, "Here, let's do this." Gerry was astonished to feel the cold rubber of Lex's butt plug against his hole. It was smooth, evenly flared. As Lex pushed and pulled, the plug slipped in deeper. Gerry liked the pressure against his prostate gland. His semi-hard dick dripped with more precum that hung like a thin spider web from the tip. Each time Lex pushed, the plug went a tiny fraction of an inch deeper, and Gerry's hole grew a little looser.

Lex said, "Take a big whiff."

Gerry felt the pulsing, pounding rush of the poppers and a jolt of pain. Lex had pushed the butt plug past the wide spot. With a snap, his hole closed around it, sucking it further inside him. Before Gerry could protest, Lex pulled it out. Gerry felt a draft in his hole. Then blam! Lex shoved it in all the way. Slurp! The plug came out. It felt so good that Gerry felt his spent cock swell anew. He could have let Lex do that for hours, but he wanted him inside him. And, to his surprise, he wanted Lex to get off. He cared that his friend hadn't yet busted a nut. He wanted Lex's cum inside him.

"I'm ready."

Lex set the butt plug aside and guided Gerry's hips until they were positioned over his throbbing cock. Gerry held the head and squatted. It slid inside him easily. He stood, turning to face Lex.

"I need to look in your eyes."

Lex nodded and lay back on the bed, his cock throbbing in the air. Gerry stood over him and put the head back inside. He slid easily down until Lex hit the back wall. Gerry twisted his hips, took a huge hit of poppers, and when the rush came, sat until the head popped through his inner hole. It felt good, better than with Norm. He placed his knees to either side of Lex's hips, lowering himself further. At last, he sat in his friend's lap, wriggling to get the last inch of cock inside him. He bounced up and down on Lex's long, fat cock, letting it slip and slide in his greasy hole. He locked eyes with Lex. He could see his backlit frame reflected in Lex's eyes. Then he saw past the reflection. There was a spark in there. He knew Lex saw the same in him. This was love. It had to be. Filled with cock, staring into his friend's loving eyes, heart overflowing, he felt that momentary flash that we feel only a few times in our lives, where everything is illuminated and sparkling. The room filled with a psychic white light, and then it was gone. It was the best moment of his life thus far. It got better when Lex pulled him to his lips. They embraced, letting their breath mingle again, tongues touching, wrestling for space.

In a smooth motion, Lex rolled Gerry onto his back, legs thrown over his shoulders. Gerry bent at the hips, letting his knees drop towards his ears. He wanted Lex close.

"Are you ready?" Lex's voice trembled with anticipation.

Gerry smiled. "I've never been more ready."

In long, loving strokes, Lex fucked Gerry with a tenderness that Gerry had yet to learn. The thrusts were gentle but firm. The technique was something only a married man could know. It came from many years of connectedness to a person. No matter that it had been a woman; Lex truly knew how to fuck. It made Gerry feel soft and pretty. Not in a shameful way, either. It was relaxed, luxurious, mellow, and soothing. As Lex's big cock slid through him, it felt like a healing massage inside him. It warmed his heart. Then Lex kicked it up a notch.

The thrusts were faster, harder. The two men both broke a sweat. Gerry's cock throbbed in the space between them like a charmed cobra weaving to the flute's tune.

Lex lowered his body, pressing the cobra between their chests. His thrusts filled Gerry inside as Lex's body slid over his cock. They grew faster as Lex breathed heavily. Puffs of air rushed past Gerry's ears. It was the sound of sex.

Gerry's cock began to throb with that familiar tingle. Lex was getting him off just by rubbing chests.

In a synchronous moment, Lex said, "I'm close."

"Me, too."

Lex was in the home stretch. He pounded Gerry hard, momentarily losing himself in wild abandon. The friction was intense, both inside and out. Gerry's balls gurgled in preparation for another massive orgasm.

"Oh, shit! Gerry! I'm coming!" They were in perfect sync. Just as Lex came inside him, Gerry splattered sperm on his chest, chin, and face. It coated their sweaty bodies, growing sticky as they rested.

The sun set outside. The two lovers were still in a wet embrace. Lex grew hard inside Gerry. They fucked again.

Afterward, as they lay on their backs, breathing at the ceiling, Lex turned to Gerry.

"Do you want to do it again?"

Gerry said, "Every day from now on."

WEE DOBBIN

BY PETER SCHUTES

Wee Dobbin roved the streets of London collecting "pure" - a polite term for dog droppings. He roved the streets with a cloth-covered bucket, collecting stool from the margins of the cobblestoned streets. The tanners used pure during the last stages of curing leather. When his bucket was full, he would bring it to the tannery in Bermondsey and collect his sixpence. With that, he'd spend a farthing on a steam and shower at the public bath before returning to his rooming house.

Wee Dobbin got his nickname in the shower at the Bermondsey Baths. Dobbin was already a name he'd used, as it was short for Robert, his given name but 'Wee' was a reference to his extraordinarily small penis. Dobbin had disliked the attention men paid to his shortcoming, but he felt no attraction to the fairer sex, and doubted he really needed it for much anyway. He'd learned to pleasure men in the dark recesses of the steam room. It earned him no money, only pleasure. Many days he walked out of the Bermondsey Baths with a pronounced limp. He had as many as ten cocks a night there before returning home to his squalid cube of a room to crash on the threadbare mattress.

London was paradise, a city filled with opportunity

and sex for a young man like Dobbin. His short nose and ruddy blond hair were a magnet for older men whose wives neglected their needs. In the baths, he'd intercept their seed, preventing another hungry mouth from entering the world unwanted. He lived to serve these needy men in whatever way he could. He preferred it in the bum, but he sometimes got so many demands for his mouth, that he could skip supper. Semen was so much more nutritious than a stale crust of bread. His nose had learned to ignore the odor of dog feces but still could detect that faintly sweet, acrid odor of cum as it leaked into his pants during his walks home from the baths.

Wee Dobbin had managed to save enough money to live a better life, but he had grown fond of the rooming house and its proximity to his cock hunting grounds. He ate humbly at an Irish tavern. Tea, eggs, and toast for breakfast, and an afternoon sandwich from a street vendor who didn't mind selling lunch to a chap who smelled of shit. He made sixpence a day, six days a week, and spent far less on his room and meals. Not bad for a shit collector!

To keep his savings from overflowing from behind the bricks, he occasionally took a purse full of sixpence to market and exchanged them for shillings and crowns. It was on one such trip that he met with a strange fate. Stepping into the street, he was nearly struck by a passing carriage. As he fell to the ground, his purse burst open. With horror, he watched several month's earning roll into a sewer grate. He gathered what he could, cursing under his breath.

Just then, a man known at the baths as "Longcock Tom" came around the corner. Longcock Tom (Lanky Tom in polite company) was a tosher, a man who sifted through sewage in search of treasure. Because of careless fools like Dobbin, there was plenty of treasure to be found down there. Dobbin recognized good luck when it crossed his path.

As Tom helped Dobbin to his feet, he said, "What happened to you?"

Dobbin shrugged. "I lost a fair bit of coin down that sewer grate. Do you know how to get down there?"

Lanky Tom playfully hefted his sizeable meat and winked. "I'll show you if you give me a double helping next time at the baths.

Dobbin couldn't get enough of Lanky Tom's fucking. Still, he hesitated, as though pondering it. By acting as though it were a chore, he would increase the value of his sexual services. He wanted Tom to feel like he was getting a bargain, even though Dobbin would have given himself to the man three times in exchange for no favor at all.

Toshers, like Pure Finders, were solitary workers. They knew each other by sight, but like gold prospectors in California, they worked as far from one another as possible to avoid turf battles. It was only after a day's gleaning that they would converge in the baths and share their stories.

Tom was the tosher who first told Dobbin the legend of the Queen Rat. The sewer folk passed this story down through the generations, probably all the way back to Roman times. In the sewers, it was said, there was an invisible woman that followed the toshers around. If she fancied one of them, she would appear to him as a lady, more beautiful than any princess, and demand his services as a lover. If you refused her, it would bring very bad luck. In truth, she was a rat that could take human form. You might realize it if she bit you during sex. Or maybe her eyes would catch the torchlight at just the right angle and glow like an animal's. Or perhaps you'd notice the claws where she should have toenails. Otherwise, you'd never know she was anything else but the most beautiful woman you'd ever hope to fuck.

It was a tall tale, but many of the toshers at the baths claimed to have seen her and given her what she demanded. They spoke of the terrible luck that befell Wall-Eyed George. Apparently, he'd been so eager to fuck her, he came before his pants were down. She bellowed a curse and shrank to the size of a rat, leaving the man staring in disbelief. Then the bad luck came. One of his sons fell from a barge and drowned. His wife and eldest daughter succumbed to an ordinary flu. It was only when the woman appeared again that he was able to break the curse. This second time, fear delayed his sexual response, and he was able to bring her to orgasm before his own. He has a new wife. His son and two remaining daughters have all found respectable professions and will be able to support him in his dotage. The luck of the Queen Rat is great when it's good, and terrible when it's bad.

So with that tall tale in mind, Lanky Tom said to Dobbin, "If ye come across the Queen Rat, may God have mercy on your soul. There's no way a wee lad like you could satisfy her." He gestured toward Dobbin's crotch.

Dobbin blushed and said, "I wouldn't want her even if I had a cock like yours. I am built exactly as God intended to serve men like you."

Tom chuckled. "Let's go get your lost coins."

About a quarter mile from the sewer grate, there was a crumbling building where Glengall Road met the Thames. They entered the dilapidated brick structure and climbed down a stone stairway to a giant hole that led, at a slope, into the sewers. Tom wore a lantern strapped to his right breast. He struck a match. The lantern beam was barely enough to light the way. A seasoned tosher like Tom had no trouble, but Dobbin struggled to keep upright. Tom held him by the hand, which helped some.

Tom knew all the twists and turns to get back to the grate. Deftly, he navigated the dark passageway until in the distance, Dobbin could make out some rays of gloomy London sunlight pouring down from above. It was the very same hole that had eaten his coins. As Tom bent, the lantern shone on the disgusting muck at their feet. Lying atop the shit was a dozen or more six-pence. Dobbin and Tom gathered them, returning them to the purse. The purse was still light a few coins.

With the expertise of a seasoned tosher, Tom raked his fingers through the waste, gathering more coins to add to the stinky collection in Dobbin's coin satchel.

"Keep those, Tom. As a token of thanks."

Tom said, "I already arranged payment at a future date. These are yours." And he tossed the last filthy coins in.

Just then, a mighty roar filled the air.

"Who goes there!? Who be toshing on my turf?"

Out of the shadows, a massive beast of a man emerged, fists clenched, muscles rippling from head to toe. The faint lamplight betrayed the handsome angles of his angry face. He strode towards the two men.

Tom said, "Run!" It was clear they were no match for this monstrous devil. But as Tom turned tail and scampered off, Dobbin missed his step for the second time that day and fell into the muck. This time, he held his coins close. Scrambling to get to his feet, he felt a mighty paw grip the back of his pants and pull him to his feet. He was face to face with the incarnation of a god. He stared into Dobbin's eyes.

"You're a beauty. What are you doing in the sewer, dear boy?"

Relieved by the gentle tone, Dobbin said, "I lost some money and my friend helped me find it."

The man smiled. "I've found a treasure myself. I can see it in your eyes. You want nothing more than to please a fellow like me, right?"

The giant man held Dobbin's head to his massive chest, letting the young man inhale the odors of maleness and sweat. It was like chloroform. Dobbin felt his head spin from desire.

"Yes, sir," Dobbin said, "I'm here to serve."

"Good. Let's go to my place so I can clean you up, and then we'll see what you're serving and how well."

After what felt like an hour, twisting and turning through the labyrinth of sewers beneath the feet of Victorian Londoners, a faint light appeared. As they drew close, it became apparent it was a sub-basement lit by a thick tallow candle.

Dobbin followed the hulking man up the stairs to a well-appointed basement. He'd dare say it was a palace in comparison to Dobbin's little room at the boarding house. There were hot and cold running sinks, maid's quarters, and even gas lamps. The man lit a lamp, bringing the whole basement into view. It stretched hundreds of feet in every direction. Dobbin couldn't imagine the house that sat on top of such a palatial cellar.

"You'll find clean clothes in there after you've bathed." He gestured to a wardrobe next to a full bathroom. The tiled floors gleamed, reflecting the soft afternoon light that filtered through the high windows at street level above.

Dobbin was baffled. Who was this tosher? What did he want?

"Let me help you." The man unbuttoned Dobbin's filthy shirt and peeled it off of him. He whistled.

"If you weren't a boy, I'd say you were a flat-chested beauty. But I prefer boys."

Dobbin warmed at the compliment. He was proud of his graceful, feminine body.

Dobbin said, "Sir, do you want me to remove my pants?"

"Sir? I do like the name Sir, but you can call me Rod. And you are?"

"Dobbin, sir."

"Short for Robert?"

Dobbin nodded.

"There's nothing short about my rod, but it is the nickname for Roderick. I'm Lord Roderick Entwhistle. Welcome to Entwhistle Manor. Now kindly remove your shoes and pants. I want to see what I'm getting."

Dobbin kicked off his shitty boots and unbuttoned his woolen pants. Aware of Rod's attention, nay, salivation, Dobbin took his time removing them, letting the huge muscular beast appreciate every angle and curve of his gracile form. He noticed Rod's massive hand as it clutched his crotch. He stroked a noticeable lump. As his hand slid downwards, Dobbin gasped. The lump went many inches down Rod's leg.

"I hope you're experienced. We'll soon find out."

Dobbin had never turned down a man before, but doubt clouded his mind. Could he handle something that size?

As if reading his thoughts, Rod said, "Many men have tried, but few have been able to please me. I have high hopes for you. If you can take me, the reward will be great."

As Rod spoke, a faint light glinted in his eyes."

Dobbin said, "Reward? I ask for no reward. What you give me in bed will be prize enough."

Rod's face brightened. "You're the first lad to say such kind words. We'll see if you still stand by your words after I disrobe."

Dobbin smiled. It was the smile that had momentarily captured the hearts of many bathers in Bermondsey. It had an effect on Rod, whose pant leg strained against a sudden throbbing.

"I'd better get these off before you trap me inside! Go draw your bath, I need a moment to cool down."

Dobbin had never seen a bathtub in a private home, let alone in the basement. Lord Entwhistle was a man of great means. The hot water fogged the mirrors that surrounded the gigantic tub. It was not the tepid water that dripped from the showers at the bathhouse. This was proper hot water. He had to turn on the cold tap to keep the water from scalding.

Dobbin slid into the tub, letting the perfectly warm water surround his dirty body. He lathered with a lavender-scented soap bar. It smelled like rich people.

The bathroom door opened, and Rod stepped in. He wore large slippers and a white robe that could scarcely cover his enormous manhood. The cock peeked out between the gap in the front. As Rod surveyed Dobbin's body, his cock began to rise, opening the robe wider.

"I love nothing more than a lad with a tiny knob. You're perfect, you know that, right?"

Dobbin smiled again, causing Rod's cock to lift further skyward. Dobbin doubted his abilities as he saw Rod grow longer and larger around with each pulse. It was easily twice as big as Lanky Tom's. Until then, Tom had been the king of the cocks. Rod had just overthrown the kingdom.

The massive nobleman stood so Dobbin's back was to him. He kicked off his slippers and dropped his robe. Dobbin couldn't see, but he heard the sounds of the clothing hitting the floor. Rod's legs entered the water first. As he sat, he pushed Dobbin forward letting his long cock rest against the boy's back. Dobbin shivered as the hairy legs enclosed him. Rod took the lavender soap and a sea sponge, scrubbing Dobbin's back in loving, gentle strokes.

Dobbin leaned back in the water to rinse. His body

rested against the powerful chest and abdominal muscles of his noble captor. He reached behind and attempted to encircle the base of Rod's cock with his small hands. The fingers barely reached halfway around. It was too big. Dobbin felt his ass muscles tighten involuntarily as though in protest. This would take all his skill. He'd never realized how excited a big cock could make him feel. It was an aphrodisiac, causing his own tiny penis to throb with anticipation while his asshole clenched in fear.

Rod picked the boy up easily and rotated him to face him. Dobbin marveled at the tower of flesh emerging high out of the water. With both hands, he stroked it, putting the tip in his mouth. It already harbored salty clear fluid at the tip. Dobbin tongued the massive slit, slurping the briny cocktail.

Rod said, "That's a good start. I have high hopes for you. Now go dry off and put on the pajamas in the wardrobe. I'll be there in a minute.

Dobbin felt like he'd walked into a tailor on Savile Row. The clothes in the wardrobe were probably worth his entire savings. Silk pajamas, wool suits, cotton shirts, and cashmere sweaters. It was an embarrassment of riches. He chose a pair of pajamas with burgundy stripes and put them on as Rod emerged from the bathroom in his robe and slippers.

Together, the two men climbed the stairs to emerge in a busy kitchen. The staff stopped what they were doing and bowed, but Rod waved them back to work.

"It smells wonderful. Carry on."

They passed through a dining room, a sitting room, a salon, then emerged into a great marble hall. Dobbin gasped at the crystal chandelier overhead. Candles had dripped little puddles of wax on the marble. The walls were covered with artwork, and the ceiling was one giant fresco. Angels emerged from clouds playing harps to the souls who were entering the heavenly gates. Saint Peter awaited with a stone tablet in hand.

Rod saw Dobbin's mouth agape. "An Italian artist painted that for me," Rod said. "You've got very good taste for a young man of your station."

Dobbin hardly noticed the classist remark. He knew he was a lowly pure finder in the presence of a god-like nobleman. It didn't bother him. He knew he would have real money one day. London was one place in the world where even a peasant could gain the wealth of kings if they were clever enough. And Dobbin was clever.

Leaving the great hall they ascended the stairs and turned right down a wide corridor. Rod stopped at the first door. "This is where the magic happens."

Dobbin gasped when the door opened. He'd never seen a bedroom like it. The bed was a sturdy, masculine work of art. It had rococo columns supporting a solid canopy of silk and wood. The bedspread looked to be woven with threads of gold that caught the light and shimmered.

"Go on, lay down, and take off your pajamas. I want to see that tiny prize between your legs."

Dobbin obeyed the nobleman. He disrobed, spying Rod licking his lips with a hunger like he'd never seen. There was no Lady Entwhistle. Rod was clearly a man's man. As he watched Dobbin, he dropped his bathrobe so that he only wore the slippers. When Dobbin lay on the bed, it hugged him. It was made from feathers and coils, the softest, most comfortable bed he'd ever known. He lay on the edge of the bed, his round, beautiful ass cheeks spread and inviting. Rod shuffled forward on his slippers until his cock found the sweet spot between the cheeks, above the asshole. He opened the chest beside him and extracted a jar filled with tallow sweetened with rose oil. He lifted his heavy cock and massaged it on the shaft, then polished the head. With the remaining fat, he inserted his finger easily into Dobbin's hole and slicked it up. Then, with the expertise of one overly endowed, he inserted a second finger, spreading them apart to stretch the hole. When Dobbin had relaxed, there was room for a third, then a fourth.

Dobbin wriggled with a heady mixture of dread and anticipation. The sweet emotions mingled in a way he'd not felt since he'd first found pleasure in the Bermondsey Baths. Lord Entwhistle's thumb was long and thick, matching his cock. Dobbin continued to relax through the pain, with a burst of pain and pleasure, the knuckles slipped past his anus. He engulfed Rod's wrist, relieved to have a reprieve from the fist. Rod pushed farther. His huge forearm muscles gave Dobbin a new stretch. It was as though he were taking Lanky Tom three times at once. Tom was long, yes, but his thickness couldn't compare to Rod's arm.

As Rod pushed and pulled, Dobbin felt sweet juice dribble from his tiny cock head. Rod scooped it up and licked his finger. His eyes closed partway as he drank in the elixir of youth. In a surprise move, Rod made a wide fist and pulled it from Dobbin's ass, quickly pushing it back in.

"Was that to your liking?"

Dobbin was still recovering from the pain, but he had to admit the pleasure was even more intoxicating. Beyond words, he nodded enthusiastically.

Rod did it again. Then several more times, until Dobbin couldn't distinguish between the pain and the ecstasy. His asshole craved flesh. He thought he was stretched as far as possible, but it wasn't so. Rod found the end of the rectum and turned a corner that Dobbin knew well. Only a few men at the Bermondsey Baths could slip past that hole using only their cocks. None had tried what Rod was doing to him now. The forearm was so thick, Dobbin feared he would split in two. He wasn't a big lad. He felt Rod's hand snake into his colon. It was a sensation like none other. Never had anything so big been inside him. But even that was about to be surpassed.

"You're ready," Rod whispered in his ear. He slowly extracted his arm. Dobbin felt an intense relief when the knuckles slipped past and his hole was empty. He bucked involuntarily as his hole snapped shut most of the way. The hole gaped with pouty lips he'd cultivated on those long nights in the baths taking cock after cock.

Rod said, "Your hole is more beautiful than any cunt. You're ready for me."

Rod stood, pulling his cock with him and slapping it on Dobbin's stomach. He took a big step backward until the head fell between Dobbin's cheeks. With confidence, Rod held the cock as far along the shaft as he could. A good five inches of hard cock hung in the air at the point past his hand. He thrust forward until his greasy cock head rested against the grey lips of Dobbin's anus. He put one foot forward and leaned into it. Dobbin saw that the cock head was as big as Rod's fist, but without a bone, it fit nicely. In a swift motion, Rod punched forward. Dobbin saw starlight dancing on the roof of the canopy. Rod's cock was not a straight cylinder. It grew thicker the whole length of the shaft so that the base was nearly twice as thick as the head. As Rod pressed forward, Dobbin's ass felt the stretch. The cock head rested against his rectum, throbbing. Rod was rock hard now. Turning the corner was going to be a challenge for Dobbin. But Rod had found others to do this with, and he knew how. Rod gently lifted Dobbin on one side giving him a near-straight shot past the second hole. But the fat cock head struggled to pop through.

Dobbin's face turned red as he fought against the pain. Then, suddenly, the massive head popped through. Dobbin began to quake. His insides trembled with pleasure. Rod kept going, stretching both the outer and inner holes until Dobbin's guts were stretched like the casing of black pudding.

Slowly, Rod pulled back, leaning onto his hind leg and bending his hips. Then he leaned forward, filling Dobbin again. He continued this rocking motion with ever-increasing intensity. Soon, his hips smacked hard against Dobbin's butt cheeks, making a clapping noise. Or was that coming from inside the second hole? It was hard to tell.

Dobbin's eyelids fluttered as he released a loud moan. He'd been fucked hard many times. He'd taken short fat dicks, and long thin ones, but never had he had one so long and fat, nor been fucked this hard. It was ecstasy. He couldn't control the muscles of his gut that contracted and squeezed Rod's mighty cock with increasing intensity.

Rod said, "You are one of those. I'm in luck." Rod stopped thrusting and let Dobbin stroke him with his insides. Now Rod's eyelids fluttered. His breathing grew fast and shallow.

"You're making me come."

Dobbin said, "I can't stop it."

Rod said, "Don't stop. Wait for it." He leaned close until his breath tickled the hairs in Dobbin's ear. Then the nobleman started thrusting again. "Oh, I'm so close."

Dobbin, upon hearing those words, felt a rising in his own loins. His tiny balls gurgled and his nub of a penis throbbed. Without any hands, only the occasional brush of Rod's abdomen as he pounded him, Dobbin came. It was the biggest load of his life. Stuffed like a pheasant at Christmas, the thick base of Rod's cock pressing against that spot near the exit, Dobbin churned out huge ejaculations that spattered his face and Rod's chest and belly.

"Oh fuck!" Rod stopped breathing for a second, then heaved a heavy sigh. Then he bit Dobbin hard on the neck. It drew a tiny drop of blood. Then his massive balls drew up. Dobbin felt them lifting off of his legs. And a heavy flow shot from Rod's cock deep inside Dobbin. It was the first time he'd ever felt the warm comfort of a man's semen so deep in his gut. Still contracting inside, his soft muscle tissue nursed more and more cum from the man's gargantuan cock.

Dobbin felt a trickle of blood on his neck. It was almost as if an animal had bitten him. He looked into Rod's eyes and they kissed. Dobbin rubbed the soft fur growing from the man's back. He caressed the man's powerful buttocks that had thrust so hard inside him. After many minutes had passed. Rod stood and stepped back until his semi-hard cock slipped out of Dobbin and smacked against his knee. As Dobbin looked down to gaze at the marvelous cock that had filled him, he saw something startling. In his frenzy of fucking, Rod had stepped out of his slippers. His toes were not toes; they were claws. Rod saw the look of shock on Dobbin's face.

"You've found my secret. Is it horrifying? Are you disgusted?"

Dobbin shook his head. It was the best sex of his life. So what if Rod Entwhistle was a rodent? King Rat.

"I wouldn't trade you for the world."

Rod beamed. "And you shall be rewarded for it. For this house is not mine. I live here, but it belongs to the first man who can take me, then refuses to reject me. Dobbin, this is your home now."

Dobbin's eyes filled with tears.

Rod said, "What's the matter, son? Have I said something to upset you?"

Dobbin sniffed. "I, uh, I never had a cock so huge. The sex was better than anything before. And you're such a lovely man. Why must you be a rat? Will I ever see you again?"

Rod smiled. "I'll come to you every night and have my way with you if that is what you desire."

Wee Dobbin smiled, wiping away the tears. "I think I found heaven."

DARK AS A DUNGEON

by Peter Schutes

❦ I ❦

SHORTY

The life of a coal miner comprises 50% labor, 35% sleep, 10% traveling in or out of the ground, and the remaining 5% bathing, eating, drinking, and whatever else he can squeeze into such a short period. It doesn't leave time enough for making babies and such, so many miners are desperate for release. They try all kinds of tricks to get at the true pleasures of life.

That twelve hours of labor, that's non-negotiable. The whole time you're in the dark, you fear for your life. You can't stop to fart around. You don't even eat unless you want to taste a ham and anthracite sandwich. So those twelve hours belong to the company and no one else.

Now, it takes up to an hour to get from the surface to the bowels of the mine and slightly longer to get back up. That time is spent in a wagon or a cage with four to six men. There isn't scarcely room to turn your head, so everybody is pretty much trapped on the conveyance. A man can't find release in that situation unless he convinces everyone on board that it's worth risking their lives to get their needs met. I learned some crews do exactly that. Each one grabs hold of his neighbor's prick, sending white rain falling into darkness two or three times before they reach the end. Those men are practical. They make good use of their time. Their wives don't know, and neither does the boss.

The sleep hours can be cut short for baby-making, but it's dangerous, too. A miner who hasn't slept enough can get himself and a whole bunch of others killed.

So we get to the 5%. Until a recent strike, the Cumberland and Partridge Joint Mining Company (CPJMC) had two showers for over a thousand men. Men walked home covered in coal, and their wives hosed them down in the backyard. Then came the big strike, and among the many compromises that worked in our favor, the CPJMC agreed to build a proper shower room like they have over in England. That strike and the events surrounding it are where my story becomes a legend.

My name is Clarence McCool, but everyone calls me Shorty. I was a hurrier starting as soon as I could quit school in the eighth grade. A hurrier is a little guy who can work in stooped, narrow tunnels. He is usually a young boy like I was, but some of us don't grow so tall, and we keep at it when we're grown. That's what happened to me. I was nineteen years old when we had that strike, and I was not much taller than the eighth graders. Didn't have any experience with sex, neither, and here's why.

When puberty came, I didn't grow like the others. While my friends were growing taller, I was just getting longer and thicker down there. All those extra inches went below the waist. I was bashful, and this didn't help any. I did my best never to let anyone figure out what had happened. Girls wouldn't want to marry me, not with what I had between my legs. So I figured out what to wear and where to put it so no one ever saw I was a freak of nature.

It turns out that this problem changed the direction of my whole life. Here's when it started: A few weeks before the strike, many miners were away at Union meetings, so the trip to and from the surface was getting shuffled around. Crews were missing a member, so they added hurriers to complete the six for the trip down or up. I got put in a cage with five men who had worked together for I don't know how long.

They were one of these groups that I mentioned that had an "arrangement," and I was gonna be in the way of their pleasure. So they were really direct with me about it.

A tall, skinny fellow named Levon leans to me and says, "We do the circle jerk, and it ain't optional."

I gulped. "Why not? You don't need me." I was sexually disabled, and I didn't want these men to learn so much about me. I hear guys talking about white rain and 'coming,' but I don't ever touch myself down there except to pee. I'm afraid it will get even bigger.

We were starting to go down, and the light was fading. A red-bearded hillbilly named Sam chimes in, "The whole cage could tip if we don't all work together, Shorty."

I really hadn't thought about it. Gravity is a bitch. So I heard all the belts unbuckling and all the zippers going down. Levon took my hand and put it on his dick. It was a lot bigger than I expected. It was a relief to hold another big one...but I was in a league by myself. Levon was not a freak, just big.

Sam undid my belt and yanked my trousers partway down. They hadn't come anywhere far down enough to release my dick. It was trapped under my belt about halfway to my knees. Sam swatted at the air near my crotch and couldn't find a dick where it ought to be. "Shorty, you got no dick? You a woman?"

If they could see me, they would know I was embarrassed and furious at the same time. I kept my cool. I thought to myself, "They can't see, so hopefully, they won't see how big I am." I took Sam's flailing hand and put it at the base of my soft cock. I was still too nervous and scared to get hard. But even soft, I just look unnatural, like an elephant trunk with no tusks.

Sam groped downward, looking for the end of my cock. "What the--?" Sam was running out of space to keep leaning. I grabbed his head and whispered to him, "Please don't say anything."

Sam was on a mission to free my cock from my pants. He was pretty rough, trying to double back my dick so he could get it over my belt. I started to complain but thought better of it. With a final tug, the whole length of my dick was liberated from my jeans and coveralls.

"Holy fuck! Shit!" Sam couldn't shut up. "Shorty has a goddamn boa constrictor in his pants! Fuck! It's too heavy to lift."

The cage riders chuckled, thinking Sam was just teasing me about a little dick.

Sam leans to Levon and says, "I ain't kiddin'. Touch it." Levon took his free hand and found my dick.

"Holy Christ! Shorty. Your dick is soft, and it's, it's...incredible."

Levon was a lot gentler than Sam. He lifted my semi-hard dick into the air. He shifted his weight so he could bend at the waist and put the head of my dick in his mouth. It felt good.

Somewhere behind me, an old man yelled, "Hey! You're rattling the cage! You want to get us all killed?" Levon let my stiffening cock slip from his lips. It swung like a grandfather clock and smacked into Sam's knees. My only consolation was that we were in total darkness. No one had seen my deformity.

Then, even though it's not allowed, Sam turns on his headlamp and points to me and my unnatural appendage. "Hell! You gotta see this."

I heard little shuffling noises behind me, and a gang

of old miners were peering over my shoulders at my incredibly embarrassingly huge dick.

"It's magnificent!" I heard someone say.

"The Lord giveth, and the Lord taketh away."

By now, I was just steamed. These old mine trolls had no right to look at me down there. I kept it hidden all these years so my secret would be safe. If there was a way to tip the basket and send every last one of those perverted old men falling a thousand feet, I would have done it right then.

I grabbed my dick and started stuffing it away. I shouted loud enough for other cages to hear, "Looks like the Lord tooketh away from all you little tiny dicks!"

The whole cage roared with laughter. Was something I said funny? I didn't think so.

"I can't help it. Stop making fun of it. It's not my fault."

"Shorty, you have been blessed." I don't know which old man said it, but there was a chorus of agreement.

"Blessed? It's a monster that scares away pussy. I will never have children."

"Sure you will. There's plenty of women that love big dicks." That was Levon, so at least he had a right to say it.

I asked him, "You think there's anyone out there who would let me fuck them? They would have to be built different."

Levon chuckled. "Women, men, they are all gonna want some of that, trust me."

"Men?"

Sam said, "Fuck yeah. Here." He grabbed my dick gently this time. He turned his back on me and maneuvered my head up to his butthole.

"What are you doing?"

"You...a big favor."

He licked his hand and wiped it on his butthole. He

applied a lot more spit to my rapidly hardening cock. As my dick grew, the gasps of surprise all around me sounded like a bad dream. I couldn't stop growing. I was growing right into Sam's shitter. He couldn't escape...he was pressed against the cage wall. I leaned back, trying to extract myself, but Levon pushed my ass forward, driving me an inch or two deeper into Sam.

More gasps. It was like being in a play and not knowing any of the lines.

Sam was making strange grunting noises that were hard to interpret. He let out a yelp of pain as he pushed back towards me.

"Sam, are you okay? Am I hurting you?"

"Yes, it hurts like hell. Now fuck me!"

He reached behind and tried to pull me towards him, but I had another seven inches to go, and he couldn't quite reach me. Levon pushed me much harder this time, and I felt my dick hit the back of Sam's poop chute. I still had four or five inches to go.

"I can't go deeper," I said.

Sam coughed and spluttered, saying through gritted teeth, "You wanna bet?" Then, he performed a miracle. It was as if he opened a side door and ushered my dick through into another room. I went all the way in. I really didn't want to lose my virginity to a red-bearded hillbilly coal miner, but that's how the cards fell.

One of the old guys behind me said, "Now, don't start swinging your hips, or we'll all crash!"

Sam said, "Don't worry, I got this." And he did. He clamped down on the base of my dick and squeezed it rhythmically. It felt like I died and went to heaven. We were both standing stock still. He unclamped and slid back and forth so that my cock head was leaving and re-entering his private room. It felt incredible. Despite the many distractions and unpleasant people around me, Sam had figured out how to stroke my dick with his insides.

I moaned quietly. Levon put one of his big hands down my chest and touched my nipple. It caused me to jerk involuntarily, and all the old men started the danger cry.

"Watch it, kid! You're gonna get us killed!"

I didn't give a flying fuck. I was too immersed in unexpected pleasures even to hear them, let alone acknowledge them. Levon kept playing with my nipple, which sent fiery electrical signals to my balls. He switched to the other nipple, and the electrical signals traveled from the base of my cock to the tip. It was as if Sam could feel the pulse because he began clamping and unclamping in rhythm with it.

And then, suspended hundreds of feet above the mine floor, at nineteen years old, I had my first orgasm. It started with the electrical pulses from my nipples. They caused me to jerk and thrash.

"Somebody hold him. He's about to blow his load in Sam."

Levon held me close, and the other three old men held my waist, legs, and abdomen. Sam used his skills to pull me gently in and out of the second chamber, tickling my head like he had a tight vagina deep inside his ass. It sent me over. I was immobile, held tightly by the four men. Levon kept fiddling with my nipples...to the point that I could barely see. So much blood was flowing to my cock, stretching it thicker and deeper inside Sam, that I may have gone unconscious for a moment. Consciousness returned and focused itself on my sex organ...I was confused by the next wave of sensation because it was my first. I suddenly felt like I had to pee, but no pee was coming out. But then my balls began to churn, and I felt an internal pump fire up. The next thing I knew, I was releasing hot liquid inside of Sam. But it wasn't pee, of course.

As that first load shot out of me deep inside Sam, I felt a euphoria I could have never imagined. Every nerve in my body was humming with electricity. Being held so still by the men was almost torture because every nerve cried out for me to pound my way deeper inside Sam. But I couldn't, and Sam was in charge.

I couldn't tell how much liquid was pouring out of me, but it felt like it could fill a coffee mug. The ripples of sexual energy grew farther apart. The climax had passed.

Sam was using two fingers to play with his little pink dick...jerking softly and rapidly. I stared in fascination and envy at his small, beautiful penis. It looked like it might be too small to make babies, but I knew Sam had a wife and baby at home.

The old, cranky men started to make noise. "Hurry up, we only got a few minutes!"

I tried to pull out of Sam, but I was still hard, which meant that I was stuck up inside him. There was nowhere for him or me to go that could separate us. I was trapped inside Sam.

Watching him play with his little dick was making me even harder. I turned to Levon and asked him to stop playing with my nipples. Another two minutes had passed, and I was still rock hard. I could see the lights of the mine floor beneath us. We were going to get in big trouble.

Worrying about losing my job and the bad breath coming from one of the old guys combined to take my mind off Sam's pretty little dick. I grew softer. I focused on the bad breath, and it accelerated the process. My dick was shorter now but not short or soft enough to extract from Sam's butt. Then, I felt an exciting, nasty sensation. Sam's ass muscles were trying to shit me out. Oh god, it felt so good; I was afraid of getting hard again.

I whispered to myself, "Bad breath, bad breath, keep your job, keep your job."

Sam grunted and pushed out as his fist flew furiously back and forth. Suddenly, I felt my cock fold on itself like soft-serve ice cream. Sam shitted my dick. As the last three inches came flying out, he suppressed a scream and shot semen straight overhead; it landed on all of us.

"Oh fuck Shorty! You are going to make so many people happy with that thing."

Now that he was no longer skewered like a corn dog, Sam turned around and planted his lips on mine. I liked the feel of his scratchy red beard as he worked his tongue into my mouth. Out of the corner of my eye, I could see we had less than a minute until we were on the mine floor.

I didn't want to stop kissing Sam, but the miners separated us. Somebody yanked up my pants and buttoned my coveralls. Sam needed help. He was feeling faint. I pulled up his jeans, turned off his headlamp, and in the faint light coming from the mine floor, I was able to button his coveralls before we landed.

When the cage touched down, we all took turns smacking Sam. His eyes fluttered, then he looked at me with a crooked grin and whispered, "Shorty, you fucked me good."

❧   2   ❧

MOOSE AND HIS FRIENDS

I never did get assigned to that cage again, so I wasn't able to revisit cage sex with those fellas. But Sam had awakened a feeling in me of pride and bravado. I had a huge fucking dick, and that made me special, not ugly or deformed. It was like a light turned on. All the shame I felt had kept me from enjoying one of man's greatest pleasures. I had never wanted to touch my massive cock because it horrified me. I had never ejaculated. Just thinking about Sam helplessly impaled on my too-big dick made me want to rub myself to orgasm...which turns out is the 'jacking off' that I heard mentioned in whispers but never discovered until now.

At home, I took every available opportunity to re-live that moment.

I shared a trailer with Earl and Jody, a childless husband and wife. They were home a lot. Earl was pretty handsome for an older guy. I think he must have been twenty-seven. He didn't work in the mines, but he had muscles like a miner. He lifted weights in the carport. I had my own room with a shower. I had to take long showers or wait until both Earl and Jody were gone to explore my new-found instrument of delight. It was so heavy that I had to be careful in the shower, or else the whole trailer would start rocking. I discovered all sorts of places on my body that increased pleasure, like the ridge between my ass and my balls and the spot about two inches inside my butt. Maybe that spot worked a lot better on Sam because even after many attempts, I still couldn't get more than one finger up my butt to touch that spot. Anything larger caused horrible pain. How he could have put my whole penis in his butt was baffling. Maybe some men are like girls, and their ass feels good when it has a dick in there. But mine? I screamed in pain with a carrot. How in hell did Sam handle my mammoth cock?

A week later, the strike came. Suddenly, none of us had a job. We walked in endless circles in front of the mine, carrying signs and demanding justice.

As I walked the picket line, I spied a few men whispering and pointing at me. I was pretty sure I knew what they were saying. A few weeks earlier, I would have died of embarrassment. Now, instead of shame, I felt pride. I shortened the length of my stride so others could pass me. In a minute, those men had caught up to me in the picket line.

"Afternoon, gentlemen."

"Hey, Shorty."

Most miners knew my name, even if I didn't know theirs.

"I sure hope this strike ends soon."

"Yeah. Money's tight."

There were three miners. One was my height and might have been a hurrier. One guy was all muscle, with arms the size of legs. The third guy was a Puerto Rican from New York named Willy. He had pretty big arms like his friend but wasn't as massive.

I extended my hand and said, "Hey Willy! How you doing? Who are your friends?" Willy perked up when I called him by name. He seemed flattered, like Johnny Cash was inviting him up on stage.

The short fellow said, "I'm Fred, and this is Moose."

I shook first Fred's hand, then felt my hand crushed in Moose's. We walked together in silence for a couple of minutes before Willy broke the ice again.

"Shorty, I heard you got a real big dick."

The other two men laughed, but their laughter couldn't make me feel shame like it might have done before. I stood straight and put my hand on my crotch, outlining it for them...reaching towards my knee.

"Yep, I sure do. Why?"

Willy was on the spot. Fred stepped in, "We was hoping maybe we could see it."

"Just see it?"

Moose nodded. "Yeah, if it's okay with you."

It sounded odd, like I was a zoo animal. I probed a little deeper.

"And that's it? Nothing else? You just wanna have a look-see at the biggest dick in Harlan County, Kentucky?"

They all three nodded, but the way they each looked to the side, I knew this could be the start of a really interesting afternoon.

"Hey, I'm happy to oblige. How will this work?"

"We share a trailer. You can come over. We can't pay you or nothing," Fred said, "But we can make it worth your while."

I was shocked. Money had never even crossed my mind. But making it worth my while sounded pretty good. I toyed with them further."

"Worth my while...you cooking dinner?"

Moose shook his head, "Nah, Shorty, nothing like that."

I shrugged. "Let's blow."

Moose drove a brand new midnight blue Plymouth Satellite convertible, a beautiful car. In a few minutes, we were at their double-wide trailer on a hillside lot in the pines. It was a nice place.

Fred and Moose excused themselves right away and

shut the door to the front room. Willy showed me around the place. There were two bathrooms and three bedrooms. Willy had the master bedroom. It was very sparse, just a bed, a dresser, and a few pictures and wall hangings. He had a Jesus wall clock. Opposite was a giant wooden fork that read "Puerto" and a matching spoon that read "Rico." Pictures of Willy's mother graced his dresser. "Is your dad in these photos?"

Willy shrugged and looked down. "I ain't never met him." His New York accent sounded so heavy and dark here in Kentucky.

"Willy! Shorty!" Fred called from the front room.

"C'mon," Willy said.

Sometimes, nothing you can dream up even comes close to what reality has in store for you. Walking into that front room, I felt like I had walked into a French novel. Here's what I saw:

Fred was naked except for girl's lace underwear and a leather collar on a leash, which Moose held in his big, meaty hand.

Moose was suspended nearly naked in some leather swing contraption that looked like it could be used for women to deliver babies. Moose's massive thighs and calves were wrapped around two of the four chains that suspended the floating birthing table from the ceiling. He wore a leather jockstrap that covered his manhood but left his butthole exposed.

Moose held a short plastic straw to his nose and inhaled some white powder from a tray. He shook his head hard, like a startled horse.

"Whoo! Yeah!" Moose sniffed the air.

"Go on, Shorty. Have a snort!" Moose bellowed.

This was a dozen new things at once. I looked at Moose holding the tray out for me. He smiled and said, "It's just diet pills, Shorty. We bought 'em at the Five and Dime."

I took the tray from Moose, whose muscles rippled

and flexed with every little movement. He was a beautiful, strong man.

Willy helped me to snort the crushed pills. He took
some and gave it back to me. "It feels better if you do it
in both nostrils."

So I did. What happened next was far more than I
could have asked for. Time shifted...shifts into now.

The powder makes me think a lot faster but worry a
lot less. It puts me deep in the moment. It also causes
some serious blood flow to my cock. Moose motions
Willy over and undoes his jeans. Willy shucks his T-
shirt. He has a great chest. I want to lick it, so I do. He
doesn't mind. I lick his brown biceps and his neck. My
dick bulge brushes against his knee, and he giggles
nervously.

Moose stuffs Willy's brown cock into his mouth and
sucks on it. It seems pretty regular at first, but Moose's
mouth is inflating it like a balloon. Willy is long. Really
long. I want to touch it, so I do. It is not thick, but it is
pretty long, with a graceful curve that makes it a little
thicker in the middle. Willy wants to kiss me, so he
does. It's an uninhibited playground.

Fred is behind me. He reaches around and undoes
my belt. He undoes the top button of my Lees and un-
zips me. Of course, nothing comes out because the end
of my swelling dick is trapped near my left knee.

Even so, the size of what they can see causes Willy
and Moose to stop what they're doing. Fred leans his
head around my torso and stares in amazement.

Moose whistles, "How long is that thing?"

I answer, "Your little slave here had better hurry up,
or he won't be able to get these tight jeans off...because
of my big fat dick."

Moose wriggles in his leather swing. He picks up a
bottle of Baby Oil off the bedside table and anoints his
body. Seeing his huge muscles gleaming reminds me of
Dolly Parton, for some reason, with her big obscene

titties. Moose is a male Dolly Parton. I wonder if he likes to be fucked like Dolly Parton, and so I ask. He laughs and makes strong eye contact with me before an emphatic nod.

Fred is still struggling to liberate my dick from my jeans. It really will get stuck if you don't do it right, so I offer to help.

Moose yanks Fred over to him and smacks him hard on his head, calling him useless. It's then that I remember Fred is wearing frilly women's panties. I thought I was the circus freak, but I was wrong.

In one swift movement, I yank my Lees down to my ankles and stand, erect.

Willy, Moose, and Fred all make the same sound... sort of like the sound a baby makes, taking in air right before letting loose with a huge wail. But these are grown men, and instead of tears, I hear envious comments. "Shit, he ain't fucking me with that thing." Willy didn't mince words.

Fred looks like a goldfish trying to catch air. Moose, who is really starting to feel the diet pills, just lets loose with a stream-of-consciousness rant about me. It sounds like, "Fuckmyeah, fuck Shorty. You're gonna poke a hole inside me with that. I want you to go in and never come out." It was pretty nonsensical, but it still sounds like I will be inserting my penis into his butt very soon. My head is spinning from the diet pills up my nose. I want to fuck everyone and everything in sight.

Moose calls me over and carefully applies baby oil to my cock. His biceps ripple as he slides his big fist up and down the obscene length of my cock, coating it with the slippery lotion. He then reaches over the mound of leather that covers his meat and fingers oil into his hole. He hands the bottle to me.

"Squeeze some up there." He stretches his cheeks apart, exposing his pretty asshole.

My mom always used baby oil for babies. I never knew it was for men's bodies and assholes and dicks. I think the diet pill powder makes me a bit clumsy. I pretty much give Moose an oil change up his ass. He wants me in him. I don't know if he has Sam's skills, but I hope so.

Fred produces an 8mm movie camera and films an establishing shot. He stops and waits for the action to start. Moose looks at me with pleading eyes and says, "Fuck me, Shorty. Don't be careful and fuck hard."

I put my giant cock head up to his hole. Lucky for us both, he's such a giant of a man, even his asshole is huge. I push in, expecting resistance, but Moose has one of those magical man vaginas that can take enormous cocks effortlessly. I slide right to the back of his long rectum. I still have four exposed inches that need to be encased in his flesh tunnel. I look up to ask him to open the side door, but he is completely engulfing Willy's long cock with his mouth. Willy pushes hard into Moose's throat; I can see the head as it moves past his Adam's apple! I probe around at the end of Moose's rectum, looking for the escape hatch. I take one heavy leg and use it to twist and adjust Moose's angle of entry. Wrong direction. I rotate him to the other side, and there it is. The second hole. Willy must have found this before, right?

I push partway past the junction, and Moose's eyes turn white. He pulls back and lets Willy fall from his mouth, and repeats, "Omifuckingod, omifuckingod. What just happened? I, I, Shorty, where is that?" Willy flashes me a puzzled look.

"It's the escape hatch. Does it hurt?"

Moose gasps and moans. "Shorty, it feels like a pussy. A pussy way up inside me. I'm gonna come from my ass!"

Fred claps his hands like a circus freak and says, "Escape hatch! Escape hatch!"

I look at him and flash a menacing grin. "Careful, or you're next."

I turn my attention back to Moose the Muscled Miner. He holds a brown vial up to his nose and sniffs. His head falls back, and I sense his sphincter and his second door go loose. That allows me to get the last couple of inches in.

I put my hand on the leather jock, hoping to see him jerk his meat.

He puts one of his giant hands on mine and pushes me away.

"Can't I watch you jack off?"

Moose moans with pleasure and says, "I don't have a dick today. Just my giant pussy. And you found a second one!"

I am usually very shy. I would never do all this with these unemployed coal miners. It must be the diet pills. They're like Spanish Fly for men.

I feel Willy behind me. He kneels to the ground and licks my asshole. This is something new. Carrots hurt, but tongues, they feel fantastic. Willy licks and probes with his long tongue, exploring my crevices. I freeze momentarily when I feel his finger go in. He pulls it out, sniffs it, and sucks on it before forcing it back inside me.

He leans forward and whispers into my ear, "Don't worry, Shorty. I can tell it's your first time. I am an expert. I will fuck you so smoothly, you won't feel any pain."

Men always make promises they can't keep.

While I'm sliding in and out of Moose's sloppy muscle hole, Willy is working a very uncomfortable second finger into my crack. Then he does a magic trick. He oils up his cock, and swaps it in for his two fingers. Yes, I see stars and groan with agony, but it only lasts a few seconds. His cock is much bigger than a carrot, but he has it lodged part way in without much pain. His head is small, and the shaft of his cock is thick in just one spot a few inches further along, so that helps. Then he holds the brown bottle under my nose, and the room begins to spin. I feel my ass go loose. So, as Willy pushes in further, I feel no stretching pain at the wide spot. Then he reaches the back and pokes me hard. That hurts.

I put my hands on his cock and maneuver it until it reaches that second doorway. I take another long whiff from the bottle. Oh, and it hurts like a motherfucker when he pushes his way in there. But then the chemicals from the brown bottle combine with the diet pills. In seconds, my escape hatch feels like a pussy, with orgasmic nerve endings that send whips of pleasure cracking through me. I pass my pleasure forward into Moose, fucking him deep and hard.

Then Willy touches my titties. He may as well have turned on a searchlight. So much heat and energy begin to course through me. I look at the ultra-masculine, muscled pussy man I'm fucking, and it gets me hot. I am overpowering this incredibly strong, thick man. He wants me to use his asshole like a pussy. He is Dolly Parton muscle man. I put my hands on his big saucer-sized nipples and play with his boobs. His big fat Dolly Parton boobs. They run slick with baby oil and sweat. I lick his smooth, bulging inner thigh, and he bucks with pleasure.

Fred films us from every angle. He spends a long time underneath me, getting shots of Willy's meat pounding into me and my meat sliding in and out of Moose. Fred has a hard-on that sticks out of his lady's panties. He is decently sized for a short guy. I'll bet he fucks Moose too. Who wouldn't fuck a muscled-up cunt like Moose? He's like a male model for hire, only free. Fucking Moose is like fucking Steve Reeves, Charles Atlas, or Johnny Weissmuller. He's a perfect specimen.

The diet pills could keep me going forever. I could fuck Moose until next week, until his ass splits open, and my dick falls off. But I feel a strong desire to have my second orgasm inside a man. And I want to time it just right, so I can take my first load of come in my ass at the same time.

I get very serious with Moose's oily nipples. I feel male energy, intense muscle energy, emanating from Moose's body. It intensifies the more I pinch and fondle his breasts. Willy is doing the same to me. I take one of his hands and redirect it from my nipple to that ridge between my balls and my ass. He knows the area. He whispers sexy lines in Spanish into my ear while he presses on it. I reach behind and press his ridge, too. My other hand floats down the front of Moose's rippled body to his belly, where I can feel, through many layers of muscle, my cock punching its way into him like a kicking baby.

At that moment, a Tesla coil of sexual energy sparks. It's dicks in asses and hands on bellies, nipples, and ridges that start a synchronized march toward simultaneous orgasm.

Moose lifts his head towards me and begins bucking in his leather swing. He stares at my crotch, watching my cock slide in and out eight inches or more, never even coming close to falling out. It is the vision he needs. I watch him moan as he puts his hand on his belly to feel the baby kick. His eyes open wide, and he says, "Oh, Shorty, I'm close! I'm gonna come. You're making me come with your big giant cock. It's so fucking big."

All this talk gets me worked up. I press on Willy's ridge to see how close he is. He says, "Oh fuck, oh shit, I'm gonna come up your ass, Shorty." And here am I, the luckiest guy with the biggest dick in Southeastern Kentucky, about to give one man an orgasm with my dick and another man an orgasm with my ass. And that makes me want to blow deep inside Moose.

Moose comes first. I watch in fascination as he cries out and shudders. From under his leather jockstrap, a small flood of semen gushes and drips. He hasn't touched himself. I gave him an orgasm simply by stretching his ass with my big dick.

Willy gets zapped by the Tesla coil of sexual energy next, and I feel hot ropes of come filling my second room. Willy just whispered in Spanish, and I think I felt tears on my shoulder, but it could have been sweat.

That leaves me. I look at the spilled semen dripping out of Moose's jock, lean forward, and taste it. It is so musky, virile, and strong. I feel Willy softening inside me, and as the pressure of his long cock subsides, I feel relief, which becomes ecstasy. I pull nearly out and then slam hard into Moose, who stares at my cock as I repeat this motion. Each time I pass his inner door, I remember how it felt to have Willy forcing past mine. I take both hands and make big boobs out of Moose's pectoral muscles. That causes him to buck, and I feel my cock grow even bigger. Moose winces at the new dimensions he's forced to accommodate. Suddenly, Willy's cock slips out of my ass, and that slick exit sends me into orgasm.

The lights in the room appear to dim. I shoot rope after rope of come into Moose, filling his ass, until come squirts out of Moose's hole past the edges of my cock barricade. These few wayward drops of semen fall onto Fred and his camera. But they are the sprinkle before the storm. I withdraw my entire cock, and with it gushes an avalanche of white semen and clear baby oil. It lands squarely on Fred's face. He smiles and laps it up while he plays with his big bulbous cock inside his lacy panties. Willy walks over to Moose and kisses him. Moose lifts a giant arm to gently hold Willy close to him. He motions me over. Moose spins me around and sucks Willy's seed out of my asshole. I wonder if I am just a one-time play toy or if I am going to become a part of this bizarre family.

After Moose drinks his fill, he turns me around again and stares at my impossibly large cock. He holds it in his hand and feels just how thick and heavy it is.

"Was that whole thing really inside me?"

I look at Willy, who is still rock-hard because of the pills. I put my hand around his cock and compare it with mine. It looks big, but it's still dwarfed by mine in length and thickness. I look at Willy and say, "I never thought my first would be so big."

Willy grins and says, "And I didn't think Moose could take that monster and live to tell about it." He flicks Moose on the nipple, and Moose wriggles with delight.

I look at Willy and ask, "So when do I get to return the favor?"

"Hell no! No fuckin way, Shorty. I am only on top." I know I'm being greedy, but it feels a little disappointing being banished from ever knowing the inside of Willy.

"I might try it." It's Fred, lying on the ground, playing with himself. I could do Fred, but not that day. I was spent.

PRISCILLA'S REBUFF

I was up for two days in a row before the diet pills wore off. I may have scared my married-couple housemates when I got a bit delirious. I jacked off a dozen times or more, trying to get to sleep. I think the trailer rocked a bit too much; nobody said anything. Finally, I slept. When I woke up 12 hours later, I had a terrible headache, and my dick felt like I had stuck it in a briar patch.

I gotta back up and explain something that will make you stop scratching your heads. My parents had me when they were really old. All my brothers and sisters were grown up when I came along. So we didn't go to church on Sunday. I never cracked a page of the Bible until college, which comes after all this anyway. I could have run around the house naked, squawking like a chicken, and my folks wouldn't have even noticed. It turns out they were both losing their memories, and if I did something naughty, they would forget to punish me. Right when I graduated eighth grade, Pa died, and Ma got worse. I called all my siblings to ask for help, but they were all living far away in big cities, and nobody wanted to come back to Harlan County for Ma. So I worked as a hurrier all day, then cared for her at night as best I could. The neighbor, Ruth Watts, would stop by and make sure Ma was okay. And then Ma went to join Pa in heaven. I was just 18, and that's when I moved in with Earl and Jody. They were like a substitute family for me.

So, nobody taught me how to jack off. Nobody told me it was an abomination for man to lie with man as he does with woman. I just knew what felt good and what I wanted to do. And sex was it.

A couple of weeks ago, I got my courage up to go over to the Watts house and have a chat with Ruth's daughter, Priscilla. I had a crush on Priscilla for ages, but I wouldn't do anything about it back then because I thought I was deformed. Now Sam and Levon had told me girls would want me even more because of my over-sized dick. I thought maybe I could persuade Priscilla to take a ride.

We were eating lemon cookies with coffee in her backyard when I said, "Priscilla, you know I have had a crush on you just forever." If she were gonna stomp on my heart, this would be it.

Instead, she said, "Really, Shorty? You're awfully cute. I didn't think you liked girls."

"Who doesn't like girls? I mean, how else would I make a baby?"

Priscilla bristled and sat up straight. I dipped my cookies in my coffee and just watched her.

"Shorty, I know you was raised by wolves, but you can't say that sort of stuff to a woman."

"Oh, I didn't know."

Men were so much simpler. It was just 'I wanna fuck you' and 'okay.' Women required a great deal of persuading, and they all wanted to hold onto their 'virtue' for some reason.

I took a different approach. "I got a big one. Biggest you ever seen."

Priscilla turned red and snapped "Shorty McCool how dare you talk to me like that!"

Like I said, women are complicated. As she scolded me, I saw one eyebrow raise a little. Was she curious?

"Ms. Priscilla, I'm sorry I don't know how to talk to you. I just know I want to be inside you."

A slap across my face, followed by a kiss on the lips, with tongue.

"Let me see this supposed big dick of yours." She was talking nasty. I wondered if I was supposed to slap her now.

We were right on the patio, where anyone could see. She took my hand and led me into the woodshed. She kept all her clothes on, but she was wearing a skirt. She put my hand up under there, and she didn't have any panties.

"Men are all liars. So if you really do have the biggest dick I ever seen, then I'll let you fuck me."

I felt something stirring down my pant leg, and I knew I needed to hurry and get it out of there before it got trapped. I unhitched my pants and dropped them.

Priscilla cut loose with a scream that could shatter windows. She ran out of the woodshed and into the house, slamming and locking the back door behind her.

It was my worst nightmare. This girl of my dreams thought I was deformed. I banged and banged on the door, shouting, "But Priscilla, you promised!"

She screamed back, "You get that monster away from me, Shorty. It ain't right. The devil made it."

I walked the 45 minutes back to the trailer with my head in a spin. I was sad, mad, and kinda glad. When I entered, the place sounded quiet. I heard Earl in the shower singing some old-fashioned song. His wife, Jody, was nowhere to be found. I sat in the living room, sipping a beer and watching the Andy Griffith show on the little TV.

Earl came out of the shower wrapped in a towel. I

startled him. I looked him over. He was pretty hand-some for 27. He graduated from community college, so he didn't work in the mines. He had some government office job in the Harlan County Courthouse. His big arms and thick legs hung off his thin body with just the right amount of body hair. His towel was hiding some-thing big, but just how big, I couldn't tell. It didn't mat-ter. He was with Jody and I did not want to come between them.

"Hey, Shorty, why you look so sad?"

"Earl, I almost had the girl of my dreams, and then she ran away and shut the door."

"What scared her off?"

I didn't feel like talking about it, so I just stood up and played show and tell. My soft dick flopped out of my jeans.

Earl stumbled backward, covering his mouth.

"Great, now I scared you too."

Earl swallowed hard. "No, Shorty, I just never saw such a gigantic cock before. I ain't afraid of it. Can I touch it?"

I shrugged. Earl lifted the head with one hand, then, when it started to slip out, he used a second hand to support the middle. He had a gentle touch. It gave me goosebumps.

I smiled when I saw the lump under Earl's towel grow.

I took back my dick and put it away on account of his being married to Jody.

While I put my meat away, Earl went and got dressed. We sat on the front porch smoking Old Gold cigarettes and talking.

"Where have you been hiding that thing, Shorty?"

"You mean 'why?' I kept it hidden under sweatshirts and loose pants and extra-long t-shirts, but the reason why is because of fraidy cats like Priscilla."

"This isn't the first time a girl rejected you?"

"Actually, it is. And I think I was right to keep it hidden from women."

"From women...and from men?"

"Oh no, Earl. Men are the best. They want to put it in their butts, their mouths; they want to put theirs in my butt...men are great. They love my big dick."

"I'm sure if you search long enough, there's a perfect girl out there for you, Shorty."

"For now, I think I'm gonna stick with men."

"Don't tell any Baptists or Snake Handlers about that."

"Why not?"

"Because they think it's a sin, Shorty."

"So, was eating that delicious apple, right?"

Earl chuckled. "Just be careful around church folk. They could get you locked up in a sanitarium for being a faggot."

I had heard boys call each other that word, but I never knew what it meant. It was supposed to be this horrible, awful thing. Sex with a man was anything but awful. Was Sam a faggot? Were Moose, Willy, and Fred faggots? Was I? Was Earl?

Earl stubbed out his cigarette and smiled at me. "God gave you a special purpose, Shorty. You need to use your dick to make people happy. Don't worry about being called a faggot by some ignorant fool. Your dick is meant to give and get pleasure. If men give it the most pleasure, then give it to men."

Earl was a Unitarian. I wonder if they all are so smart.

I noticed Earl was looking sad. I had hogged the whole conversation without asking him anything.

"Earl, you look like your mule died. What's wrong?"

Earl shrugged, sighed, and puffed on his cigarette. "Jody is at her mother's house."

"Oh, you must miss her. When will she be back?"

The look Earl gave me said everything. Jody was gone for good.

I put a comforting arm around Earl and let him cry on my shoulder. I might have asked why she left, but he was hurting too bad so I let it go. It felt nice to be there for him. I rubbed his back and let him soak my t-shirt with tears.

❊ 4 ❊
A NEW OPPORTUNITY

The strike ended with no change in hourly wage. That sounds like we lost, but it was better. Instead of 12 hours, we got an 11-hour working day, plus now we got paid for our time going down and coming back up. Suddenly, another 5% of the day was given back to the miners. There was a big baby boom in Harlan County the next year. And as I mentioned in the beginning, one of the bargaining points was the showers. If men could take a hot shower before they got home, then they didn't have to get hosed down with cold water by their wives, and that meant they were ready to make babies right away. A lot of dinners burnt on the stove after those showers were built.

Joe di Mazzo was the lone employee in charge of the old two-headed shower room. He had an easy job because only a dozen men a day came through there. He kept 30 towels and washed them every other day.

With the new construction, things were going to get very busy. The bosses knew this planned for it. They promoted Joe to manager and told him he could hire one hurrier to work under him. Joe pulled me aside and asked, "McCool, you want to work for me?"

I thought about it and said, "Yeah, if the pay is any good."

Joe grinned and said, "Moose told me you would say exactly that."

In truth, I didn't need much money because I had no grand plans. Earl and Jody were always encouraging me to get my equivalency and go to Southeast Tech, but I didn't know what for. I made $1.85 an hour as a hurrier. I was getting 12 hours of pay, but with the new rules, I would work 11 hours and get paid for nearly 13 because of the conveyance pay.

So when Joe says, "It's a split shift, morning, then night. You get $50.00 bucks a day plus breakfast and dinner."

If I had been eating cornflakes, they woulda come out my nose. I played it cool.

"So, like 6:00 am to noon, then 6:00 pm to midnight?"

Joe smiled. "More like 4:00 am to 8 am, then 4:00 pm to 8:00 pm."

If I were free from 8:00 to 4:00, I could take those equivalency classes and go to college. I would be a fool not to.

"What else did Moose tell you?"

"He said you were a hard worker. Very hard."

"Yeah, I was a hurrier since I was 13."

Joe smiled, then switched topics. "This shower room is unlike anything you've seen. There's 50 shower heads in a giant open area. No stalls or nothing. We have changing rooms over there on the far end. I don't know how it's gonna work. I need you to help me develop a proper system."

"No problem, Joe."

"And we gotta have a towel system, a shower system, a changing room rotation, and a clothing system for clean and dirty."

"Do they got them locker baskets I heard about?"

"Yeah. Each miner gets a key and padlock. He puts his city clothes in the basket, hauls it up overhead on the chain and locks it, then lowers the other basket to get his filthy coal clothes."

"So he won't need a shower then, right?"

Joe paused and smiled. "See, I need a second brain to work through this. You're right. I was trying to figure out how they would manage colliding in the showers. We don't let 'em use it until the end of the day."

I thought some more. "How about we give them a towel and a changing room key in exchange for their ID badge and their locker basket key? When they turn in a towel, we give them back their locker key. When they turn in the changing room key, they get their badge."

Joe smiled, "I didn't pick you for your brain, but you, son, are a smart young man."

"You picked me because Moose says I work hard."

Joe grinned. He was looking at my loose jeans, trying to see what Moose must have really told him.

I never really noticed Joe before. He had black curly hair, a big mustache, and Italian-style tan skin. He wore his Levi's tight. There was a big worn patch down the left side where his dick was smashed between the pant leg and his thigh. He put his left hand in his belt loop and reached down, playing with the worn spot and looking at me.

Joe wasn't exactly handsome, but he wasn't ugly.

"Real hard, right son?"

I put my hand near the middle of my dick and rubbed it a bit. Joe needed nothing else. He pushed me into his office, shut the door, and pinned me up against the wall. I wasn't sure what he wanted. He didn't kiss me, didn't touch me there, and didn't touch himself.

"What's this about, Joe?"

He got this strange look in his eyes. It wasn't scary, it was more sad.

"C-can I see it, Shorty?"

I shrugged and unbuckled my trousers. Now Joe was touching himself through his jeans and rubbing that worn spot. A little spot formed at the end. He was leaking.

I dropped my pants and then my boxer shorts. Joe gasped like a scared deer. His hand sped up, rubbing that worn spot faster and harder.

I came near him, but he pushed me back with his free hand. He pointed to my dick.

"Get it hard, Shorty."

I swung it back and forth so it was hitting me on either ass cheek. It was not fully hard, but it was longer and thicker.

"Joe, let me see yours."

He growled at me, "No! Just get yours hard!"

"I need you to suck it for me, Joe."

This made him even madder. "That is a sin! Looking at you is fine in the eyes of the Lord. But touching you is sinful."

"It feels real good, though," I reasoned. "I can't just get hard on your say-so." At least let me see your dick. It ain't no sin."

He stopped rubbing himself and opened his jeans. A big fat Italian cock came flying out, pointed skyward."

That helped, and I got hard. He carefully put it away and continued to rub through his pants. I figured out what was going through his head. He could bring himself to come if he wasn't touching flesh, just denim, and it wouldn't be a sin. I was bored as shit with this arrangement, but it was no skin off my ass to flex and make my cock bounce up and down for him.

"Shorty, do you like having a big dick?"

"Hell yeah! Do you?"

"Do I what?"

"Do you like having a big dick?"

Joe surprised me, "Mine is tiny. It's almost invisible."

Okay, he was full of hang-ups. He had a big, fat, juicy piece of meat under there. I figured he had a lot of rules about what I should say or do, so I just kept flexing my cock up and down and stopped talking unless he asked me something.

"How big is it, Shorty? Have you measured it?"

"I don't know. Almost as long as a ruler?"

"And how big around?"

These were tough questions. I found the thickest part near the base and wrapped my fingers around it as far as they could reach, then I held it up for Joe."

"Like a beer can?" Joe asked.

"Bigger, I guess, 'cause I can get my fingers to touch on a beer can."

Maybe those were the magic words. Joe bent forward, breathing through his nose really hard. He shook like he was having a seizure, and then a big wet spot appeared and spread out until the whole left side of his jeans was wet.

He went to the old shower and stood under it, soaking his jeans with water.

I pulled my trousers back up. If Joe was gonna be my boss, I hoped we wouldn't have to do this much. It didn't seem fun for him, and it was boring for me.

Joe was all business now. "New showers open next week. Ready to start right away?"

"Yes, sir."

"See you Monday at 4:00 am."

5

DROPPING THE SOAP

I know things were pretty adventurous already, but from the day those showers opened, I was on a sex rollercoaster with hairpin twists and turns.

On the first day, there was a backup because nobody read the signs explaining about the lockers. I had to walk the men through it as they came in for the early shift.

First, each man was assigned a numbered padlock. They stripped naked and put their clean clothes in one basket. Then they'd yank the pulley until the basket was high overhead and lock it. Then they put on their dirty clothes to go to work. That part was not rocket science, but it felt like I was teaching first graders how to fly a plane.

When the men came off the shift, they stripped naked and put their dirty clothes, minus the badge, into a second basket and pulled it high next to their clean clothes. The two baskets would share the padlock. The men were naked, with just their badges and the locker key. Naked, they walked over to Joe's cage, where he would hand each miner a towel and a changing room key in exchange for his locker key and badge.

The men would stand together in the hot group

showers, which ran constantly. Nobody controlled a spigot.

Soap was free, but the men seemed to run out a lot, so I was tasked with going into the mass of wet bodies to deliver bars of soap every ten minutes or so. It was pointless to wear any kind of clothes on the job, so I just wore rubber sandals. I could have worn bathers, but after years of hiding my secret, I wanted the whole mine to know about me and my beautiful deformity.

The men loved the group showers. They scrubbed each other's backs and butts and snapped each other with towels, despite the "No Horse Play" signs posted everywhere. I would have to talk sternly to anyone who disobeyed, which led to a lot of mean jokes.

"Shorty, it says no horseplay. From what I see, you're the horse!"

It was pretty fun work. Joe stayed in his cage, watching the naked men and rubbing himself. I was smack in the middle of these wet naked men, and I caused quite a stir with my big cock.

Here's what I learned about men that very first day. When they are all naked together under bright lights, they play around in a very innocent way. It's darkness that changes things. The company did a great job on the shower, but they weren't really thinking when they built the changing rooms. Once a man stepped inside, he was in darkness. And in darkness, he feels private. And he wants to do private things.

On that first Monday, a stout miner named Marty asked me to help him with his changing room door. He said it wouldn't open. I tried it, and it opened just fine. He walked in, then grabbed my dick, and pulled me in with him, shutting the door. We could see each other in the light coming through the cracks of the door. His penis was short and thick. He bent over the changing table and presented me with his ass.

"Come on, Shorty, plug me up! I'm clean up there, I made sure."

He produced a small tub of Vaseline and applied it generously to his ass and my cock. I was at full attention.

Marty steered my cockhead into his hole and sighed. I pressed forward, and he cried out.

"Shall I stop?"

"No! Keep going. Fill my ass. You have all the power."

I had to agree; I felt very powerful as I penetrated this father of five. I felt him loosen, and I seized the moment to go deeper. My cock hit the rear rectum wall. He reached back and gasped at how much cock was left outside.

"Oh, Shorty, be gentle. I'm not deep enough."

"Yeah, you are."

I fiddled with my dick until I felt that second hole. He probably didn't know about it; his short dick would have never found it on anyone.

I adjusted my angle and pushed through.

Marty screamed like a girl. "What did you do!! Did you tear me open?"

"Shh. No, I went into the next room. Is this the first time someone's visited you there?"

"Next room?"

I had studied Gray's Anatomy at the library to better understand, so I explained it while I plowed his ass.

"It's -unh - your -unh- sigmoid - unh -colon."

"Whatever it is, it feels fucking great!"

I didn't wait for permission; I just started pistoning in and out of Marty's slick butthole at a breakneck pace.

"Oh, Shorty, yes, yes, fuck me, take me, you're so powerful!"

And I did as he asked. The Vaseline made for a fast

ride. Within three or four minutes, I was shooting sperm into his colon. He stayed face down, moaning and playing with his little fat cock. As I pulled out, he shot a load on my flip-flops.

I hurriedly wiped myself down and returned to the showers, where men were barking for soap. I ran to Joe's cage, and he grabbed a few bars. I distributed them, and peace was restored. I saw Marty turning in his changing room key for his badge. He motioned me over.

"What do I owe you?"

I was taken aback by his rude question...for a minute. I wasn't sure if it was a dollar or ten dollars, so I reversed it.

"Was it worth much to you?"

"Oh fuck yes,"

"How much?"

"Shorty, the strike set me back. I only have fifteen dollars. Is that enough?"

I nodded. "Yeah, the going rate's twenty-five, right?" I was fishing.

Marty nodded. Good, I did my market research and figured out what I'm worth.

Then Marty added, "But honestly, Shorty, with that chunk of meat between your legs, you should be asking for forty."

And that was only my first day in the showers.

6

CUMBERLAND GAP

Now that I worked the showers, I got to see miners I never even knew existed. There were a lot of guys who worked the night shift and slept during the day. They got a pay differential for the hardship.

As a hurrier, I only made deliveries to a few dozen men. Now, I was at the beck and call of over 1,000 miners.

There was one miner who made my dick hard just looking at him. He had short copper brown hair, dark eyes, a red mustache, and a dick that may have been bigger than mine. I couldn't say for sure because he stayed soft. In the showers, he seemed bored and uninterested in the other men. Joe told me his name was Frank Pennington. I figured he would know. Frank was Joe's type, like me.

I don't know what it was about Frank Pennington, but his snobby demeanor made me want him more. I tried to get close with various excuses, like a fresh bar of soap, and he just looked sideways at me and pretended I didn't exist. That drove me wild.

I followed him to the changing room, but he closed and locked his door behind him. He didn't have a wedding ring. See, some people have 'types' that they are attracted to. Me, I was attracted to men, end of story. Some guys only like big dicks on guys or big boobs on women. Some like short guys, others like tall guys. Me, I like men. Short, fat, skinny, tall, big, small, eighteen to eighty; blind, crippled, or crazy. Just men.

Frank was not attracted to men at all, I figured. I was invisible to him. So was every other man in there. He didn't see Joe rubbing one out; he didn't see me with my dick halfway to the floor.

I was determined to seduce him, but I had no idea where to start. He kept to himself and didn't seem to have any friends at all. One night, after he was done, I followed him outside to spy on him. He got into a Chevy truck. There were no bumper stickers, no clues to his personality, nothing I could see from where I stood in the darkness.

But I was determined. Once I make up my mind, I'll look for answers until I know how to get what I'm after.

The next morning, I went outside for a smoke right when Frank pulled up. I walked up to him while he was getting gear out of his truck.

"Hey, Mister, you got a light?"

Frank turned and looked at me with an expression I can only describe as 'annoyed.'

"Yeah, hang on," he said and punched the lighter in his truck. When it popped out, he tried to hand it to me, but I cupped his hands in mine, so he held the cigarette lighter for me."

I smiled and said, "Thank you, sir."

He paused and looked at me, kinda strange, then grabbed his gear and slammed the truck door. I noticed he had a miniature pair of handcuffs dangling from his rearview mirror.

"Someone in your family a cop?"

He glared at me, then said, "Something like that."

And he left it all mysterious. I stood by his truck while he walked into the changing room. Once he was inside, I snooped around, looking through the windows to see what else I could learn.

On the front seat, there were two issues of *True Detective Magazine* and a can of cherry pipe tobacco. The pipe was probably in the glove compartment.

He was as mysterious as they get.

Now that I was making good money, I had some extra cash to spare. I cooked up a plan. If I had known where it would lead, I guess I would still have done it.

Joe was really keen on Frank, like I said, and he always gave him the same changing room, the only one with a blow dryer and an iron. The next night, when Frank came in, and Joe gave him his key, I walked over to the changing room and slipped a brand new copy of True Detective under the door. I waited and watched Frank as he opened the door, stumbling across the magazine. I wanted to see his reaction. He quickly turned and looked right at me. It was too late to cover it up. I wanted him to know, just not so soon.

He smiled wickedly before he shut the door and locked it.

On his way out, he grabbed me and said, "Come have a smoke."

I obediently followed him to his truck. He whirled around and poked me in the shoulder with the magazine.

"You like *True Detective*, Shorty?" Apparently, I wasn't invisible, and he knew my name.

I bluffed. "Yeah, it's cool." I hadn't even looked inside.

He opened it, thumbing through the pages. He stopped at a photograph of a half-naked lady bound and gagged.

"You like that, Shorty?"

I didn't know the right answer, so I mumbled, "Sorta."

"Do you wish you did that to her, or do you wish someone would do that to you?"

He was mean. I felt ashamed when I said, "I would let you do that to me, so long as you weren't gonna kill me."

Those were the magic words. He rubbed his crotch and put my hand on it. Under his black jeans, I could feel he was hard and very, very big.

"What time are you off?" He asked.

"Oh, um, another 45 minutes."

"I'm waiting right here for you. You want that?"

"Yeah. We going to your house?"

"Not my house. It's a little place down the highway a spell."

"Cool." I was scared, but didn't show it. This man was taller than me and bigger than me in every way. If he was a killer, I was shit out of luck.

My shift ended. Out in the parking lot was Frank, puffing on his pipe and looking at me with the hungry eyes of a bobcat chasing a rat.

I walked up to the truck, hiding my fear behind a confident swagger. Frank reached over and grabbed my left titty, twisting it hard. I yelped in anguish and surprise.

"You don't like that?" He asked.

Thinking fast, I said, "You surprised me. It felt good." Why I lied like that is just an example of how I always try to make men happy.

He reached between my legs and crushed my balls with his big, meaty hand. I smiled and pretended to like it.

"I knew you was one of us." He said. I wondered who 'us' could be.

An hour's drive with Frank down Highway 119 gave me my answer. Up an unmarked driveway was a cabin, red lights glowing from within. An older, mustached man in a black leather jacket sat smoking a cigar on the porch. Over the door was a sign that read, 'Cumberland Gap M.C.'

Frank pulled a leather jacket out from behind the truck seat. It was emblazoned with a large embroidered patch on the back that matched the sign over the door.

The cigar smoker greeted us.

"Frank, who's the fresh meat?"

Frank smiled, "Shorty, this is Dick." We shook hands. Dick blew cigar smoke in my face to see how I would react. It smelled like shit, but I just smiled and breathed it in.

Dick smacked my ass really hard, painfully hard, as I walked into the club.

Inside was a room that made Moose's front bedroom look like a church picnic. In fact, I saw Moose suspended by his ankles. A skinny man smacked Moose's cock with a riding crop. He insulted Moose as he struck him. "Big muscle man with a tiny, tiny cock. You should be ashamed"! Then he whacked him. Moose was gagged with a bandana, so he could only cry out in grunts and moans.

"Fucking little vagina dick, boy. I can't see it to hit it." He smacked Moose's dick again hard, leaving a red mark on his thigh and dick. "Do you sit down like a girl to pee?"

Moose nodded his head.

But I am not doing the room justice. There were over twenty men in various states of undress. On a table nearby, a handsome grandpa had his muscular arm halfway up someone's ass. The man moaned and hung his head. I thought I recognized his voice. I saw a red beard, and I knew it was Sam, my first ass fuck. No wonder he could take me so easily. He must have done a lot of stretching out here. Sam looked over and smiled. "Shorty McCool! Welcome!"

My name caused some murmurs and whispers to go around the room. I could only make out a few words like 'hung,' 'cock,' and 'huge.' I guess I was infamous now that I worked naked in the showers.

To tell you the truth, the place looked and smelled like how I imagined Hell to be. The moans and groans coming from different parts of the cabin only added to the feeling that these were sinners paying dearly for their crimes.

Frank steered me to a web made out of chains that stood in the center of the room. He looked me in the eyes and asked, "Do you want this?"

I couldn't keep up the charade. I wasn't going to say 'yes' to this man without any idea what I was agreeing to.

"Frank, I probably do, but I don't know what you have in mind."

He smacked me across the face and said, "Don't talk back"! I should have hauled off and punched him, but for some reason, that smack felt good.

"Yes, sir," I croaked obediently.

"Since this is your first time, you go on the web. Once you're on the web, anyone can do as they please."

"Murder?"

The whole room busted out laughing.

Frank silenced them with a hard fist to the table. "No, Shorty, not murder!"

"Okay then, I'll do it." Cheers and applause came in response.

Frank lifted my t-shirt off, pinching a nipple so hard I almost cried. Then he removed my boots. Finally, he unbuckled my belt and stripped me completely naked.

I heard whistles and catcalls:

"Fuck me, that boy is huge!"

"Look at that ass. So round and firm."

"The right height for sucking."

I felt horny now, hearing how my body excited these

men. I wondered how they were going to take advantage of me.

Click! Frank had my right wrist handcuffed to the web. Click! Click! Click! Now I was spread-eagled. Frank turned a crank that leaned the web back about 45 degrees. I leaned against the chains and waited for the initiation to begin. Fear made my dick soft.

An older man with long hair and a pot belly approached me from the front. He was already ugly, to begin with, but then he gave a big grin and slipped out his dentures, revealing a toothless maw.

"Pussy mouth! Pussy mouth!" The men chanted.

I was frozen in place. Pussy Mouth bent down and swallowed my soft cock. I mean, he swallowed it like it was a piece of fried chicken. My limp dick was surrounded by smooth, toothless gums at the base, and the head was deep inside Pussy Mouth's throat. And then I started stiffening up. I was afraid I was going to choke this toothless old man, but he had been to the rodeo a few times, and I was just a big bull to ride. He expertly impaled his mouth on my ever-growing cock. Sliding to and fro, he brought me to full tumescence.

And that was his job. He pulled away, displaying my teetering boner as if it were a sculpture he had carved himself.

A line of men formed, all anxious to experience my dick in their asses. One by one, they came and sat on it as best they could. Most shook their heads and gave up. If Moose weren't hanging upside down, I would have called for him to show these fools how it's done.

Meanwhile, in the back, a man had his face buried in my ass. I felt his rough five o'clock shadow scraping my skin raw while his long tongue probed my shitter. He finished and stood. I expected him to fuck me in the ass, but he came around and pulled my mouth onto his dick. He wasn't very big, so I could take him without choking or gagging. He fucked my face intensely, shooting his sperm into my mouth so hard that it came out my nose before walking away.

Sam came over, stretched like a worn-out sock, and slipped his gaping anus over my dick until it was buried to the hilt. Sam rode me like a pony, but he was so loose it was like throwing a hot dog down a hallway. He found the right angle for me to poke his prostate and just worked it. It didn't do a whole lot for me, but I saw his eyes roll back in his head. He moaned softly, dripping clear sticky fluid on the floor and my feet. He pounded his small penis with his fist, and within a minute or two, he came. He walked away, letting my unsatisfied cock pop out of his ass at full mast.

Out of the shadows came little Fred. He had on women's red underpants. He climbed the web and rubbed his crotch in my face.

"I knew I would have you, Shorty." His plump cock wouldn't fit into the women's panties. I felt the head rubbing across my face, leaving a snail trail of clear seminal fluid on my cheeks and lips. It tasted sweet.

Little Fred turned around. He lowered the back of his panties and shoved his ass in my face.

"Get it wet for me, Shorty."

It was a perfect little ass. It looked good enough to eat, so I put my mouth on his hole and started licking the outside.

"Put your tongue in there," Fred ordered.

I poked my tongue in his ass and licked him. He tasted like a penny. I kept going, building up reserves of saliva and injecting them into Fred's anal cavity. He was ready.

Fred grabbed the chains on either side of my head and extended his ass out until it was hovering over my towering cock. With expert aim, he piloted his ass opening to land on my cock head. He looked over his shoulder to watch the length and width of my boner invade him.

"Oh, shit! Oh fuck that hurts! Oh yeah. Oh yes. Oh yes."

Fred's cries of pain dissolved into moans of pleasure as he drove my cock deeper inside him. In a matter of moments, he was sitting on my hips, looking into my eyes.

He held onto the chain webbing with one hand and used the other to stroke his large manhood. With his feet, he rocked himself up and down on my cock. It felt good. I moaned softly with satisfaction. He just wanted to rub himself against me.

Fred had some kind of complex that came out in his filthy language. "Shorty, put it inside my pussy. Fuck my pussy! Make me a mother. Your cock feels like a baby in my birth canal! Make my pussy wet!" He stroked himself vigorously. Unfortunately, Fred was heavy on the trigger. He sprayed come on my face and quickly lifted himself off of my unsatisfied cock.

I wanted Pussy Mouth again, but he was gone. I was losing my boner. I wasn't going to be able to come like this. Or so I thought.

Frank approached me from the front and spat in my come-splattered face. I couldn't wipe it away. I had to let the saliva trail down my cheek. It should have made me feel mad or sad, but it made me hard. Frank saw this and smiled.

He grabbed my nipples in both hands and began torturing them. A light bulb went off in my dick, and I got very aroused. The combination of being bound and tortured was new to me. I didn't expect to like it so much.

To drive the point home, Frank mocked me. "Yeah, little pussy likes it, huh?"

I nodded.

Then he brought his knee up hard and connected with my balls. The pain was excruciating. I saw stars floating in front of my eyes. In any other setting, I would have lost my hardon. But enduring this pain in such a helpless pose was doing funny things to my brain. It was bringing pleasure when it shouldn't.

"Little faggot likes it when I hurt him, huh?" He punched me in the stomach for emphasis.

And I liked it. I felt ashamed of how much I enjoyed being tortured.

Frank undid his belt and took it off, cracking me in the side before walking out of sight behind me. Over and over, he cracked his belt across my ass. It hurt terribly and felt so fucking good.

There was a pause, and I heard the rustle of clothing. He must have dropped his jeans because suddenly, I felt a huge cockhead pressing at my sphincter. He didn't spit, didn't use Vaseline, he just started pushing his way in dry.

This pain was not the kind I could take or enjoy in any way. Mercifully, he pulled out and came to the front.

I got to see my torturer in his full glory. He had auburn pubic hair framing a dick that rivaled mine in length, if not width. He had taken off his t-shirt to reveal a well-built body covered in freckles. Even his enormous cock had freckles! I might have seen a little of my own blood on the head.

He grabbed my neck and forced my mouth onto his cock.

"You're drier than Crum County, so suck this good. I don't want blood on my clothes."

I liked how he managed to throw humiliation and degradation into a single command. He wanted me to be ashamed for not being naturally lubricated. It's an ass, not a pussy! But I knew better than to say anything.

I gagged and choked on his cock. He pushed it too far in, and I puked. He felt it and smacked me hard. "Swallow it"!

I wanted to spit it on the floor, but I had to swallow

the nasty burning bile. He held me where I couldn't breathe out my mouth, so I had to use my nose. The next time I threw up, it came up my nose and out my nostrils.

Frank removed his cock. He took a blue bandana out of his back pocket and wiped my nose and face. He spit into the bandana, then used it to gag me. It tasted of bile and smelled worse.

He wandered behind me and pushed his way inside me a couple of inches. I knew there were so many more to go. I was surprised by how easily he slid in. He just kept going and going, like a car full of clowns at the circus. It moved right past my rectum and into my sigmoid colon. It was easy because he was thoroughly soaked with my spit and because he was not as thick as me. It was the first non-painful sexual act he committed on me. But I knew if he thought it felt good, he would torture me some more. So I did a Brer' Rabbit.

I moaned and cried as if I were in terrible pain.

"Does that hurt, little faggot?"

I nodded my head emphatically. "You're ripping me apart."

He fucked rough, taking long, cruel strokes that did hurt, but in the good way. Each time he fucked his way past my little inner vagina, I got closer to coming. I wasn't sure how he would take it if I exhibited such obvious pleasure.

His strokes grew slower, which meant he was very close. I heard his breath change. He held my waist through the chain webbing and pulled me close. I started to drip pre-ejaculate on the floor. My cock was at full attention.

Frank smacked my ass hard, like a spanking. He kept spanking me over and over, which brought him to the edge.

Those smacks vibrated my whole body, and my dick

noticed. Suddenly, I was heading towards a no-hands orgasm with no way to stop it.

Just then, I felt Frank plunge all the way inside and stay there, gasping.

Then he came. A rushing torrent of hot fluid filled my sigmoid colon. The heat and wetness put me over the edge. I sprayed the air with my come, splattering all over the clubhouse.

Frank pulled out, bringing forth a river of his semen cascading like a waterfall to the floor. "Who's next? He's all loose and wet for you now."

One by one, men came at me from behind and fucked me. I tried to turn my head to see them, but I couldn't. Over the course of the next two hours, I got implanted with sperm from over a dozen men. Most of them were small to average, and they went in painlessly. It was the thick ones of any length that hurt the most.

One man was the thickest I had ever suffered. I couldn't see it, but it felt like a whisky bottle. It was long, too. If it weren't for all the semen lubricating my anal canal, I would have torn open. He was long enough to get past the rectum. When he did, it felt like the first time. Indeed, it was the first time anything so massive had been inside me. Willy was big; Frank was longer. But this mystery man was teaching me a lesson on how I must feel to other guys. He was careful but persistent. His gentleness was a sign of wisdom. He knew better than to injure or damage me. He thrust in and out, his impossibly thick cock forcing its way deep inside me. He was very talented. Each time he pressed in, he grunted with pleasure. One time, he caught himself and laughed softly, saying, "I'm a pig. You're my slop."

Did I know that voice? It seemed familiar. The intense pressure on my inner sphincter caused me to start dripping again. Oh, the joy of being stretched so fully in so many places! It was happening again. I was going to have another orgasm! This time, I shot my load first. Then Mr. Thick grunted and pounded harder, milking me of the last drops of my semen before he unleashed a flood inside me.

He kissed the back of my neck and whispered, "Shorty, let's do this again." He stayed inside me until his thick cock lost its hardness, and I shit it out along with a puddle of his semen.

"Who are you?" I asked, craning my neck but failing to see him.

"I'm sure you can figure it out." And then he disappeared out of sight into the red-lit room. His whisper haunted me.

The remaining men who fucked me were of no interest, but I made sure to pretend they were hurting me or pleasing me or whatever physical sensation they wanted their fucking to mean to me. I held their come inside until they were all finished.

Frank removed the gag and kissed my forehead.

"May I make an announcement?" I asked.

He nodded. The torture ritual was over.

"Hey guys, I have at least five loads worth of come in my ass that I need to release."

Sam came forward. "Can I have it?" He asked.

"Sam, it would be an honor. I want to see this."

Frank undid my cuffs. Sam lay on the ground, and I squatted over him. My huge cock brushed across his forehead and stayed there.

"Ready?"

Sam nodded vigorously.

I bore down, and a torrent of white juice poured from me. Sam caught a lot of it in his mouth and swallowed. But there was too much, and it began running all across his face, into his ears, his eyes, his nose. He was plastered in semen from a half dozen men. I leaned over and kissed him, getting a mouthful of the man broth in the process. He lay on the floor, unable to open his eyes for fear of getting the stinging fluid in there. The man who had his arm inside Sam earlier threw him a towel.

I looked around the club. Most of the men were gone. Frank offered me a ride home. My crush on Frank was over. He was handsome, but he was too violent for my tastes.

7

TRUE DETECTIVE

The next morning, Frank was right back to his snobby self. He didn't acknowledge what had transpired, and he pretended I was invisible. That suited me just fine.

I looked all around the shower room and the changing rooms trying to figure out who my mystery fuck had been. There were lots of guys with long thick cocks, and I didn't really know any of them. It was clear that Mr. Thick knew me, and I knew him. I couldn't get him out of my head. He made me feel so good. And he wanted to do it again. I debated asking Sam if he knew who it was. I couldn't ask Frank; he acted like I didn't exist. I made a mental checklist of all the miners with big dicks who I knew and who knew me.

Levon
Joe DiMazza
Frank
Willy
Fred

There were many others, but we weren't acquainted. I started with Fred. He was in the showers, washing coal out of his groin. His dick was plenty big.

"Hey, Fred."

"Shorty, how you been?"

"I enjoyed last night."

Fred laughed. "You're not supposed to!"

"Yeah, haha. I didn't see you when it was over." I was fishing.

"I left right after I got off on your face. Moose needed me to drive him. He was drunk."

No fish.

I was pretty sure it wasn't Willy, unless Willy had surgically thickened his penis. Willy was average thickness. Just to be sure, I asked Fred, "I expected to see Willy there."

Fred laughed again. "Willy would never go there. It's not his thing."

So now my list of 5 was down to 3.

I eliminated Frank because I saw him while I was getting fucked by Mr. Thick.

Joe di Mazzo had the right-sized cock. Knowing all I did about his weird hang-ups, I thought it unlikely he was the one. I needed to be sure.

At the cage, Joe handed me two bars of soap. I lingered a minute.

"What is it, kid?"

"Have you heard of any motorcycle clubhouse off of the 119?"

Joe paused. "Are you talking about the Cumberland Gap?"

"Yeah, that's it. Do you ever go there?"

"Hell no! The place is crawling with faggots."

I was startled by his response. I hadn't considered that Joe was doing all his weird stuff with not touching skin to keep from admitting he was a faggot.

"Shorty, don't go there. They'll make you a faggot like them."

"Oh, of course not. I only ask because I heard Frank goes there,"

"Frank is fucked in the head. Easy on the eyes, but dangerous." Joe was just looking out for me. He was built right, but he wasn't Mr. Thick.

That left Levon. I accosted him in the showers. "Levon, how are things?"

He smiled at me. "Good, Shorty. And you?"

I gave a grin. "I can't complain. Ever since that day in the cage with you and Sam, I have been fucking non-stop."

"Well, you definitely have all the right parts for it." Levon playfully slapped my penis shaft at the halfway mark.

I smacked him back in the same spot. "You too."

Levon soaped himself up. "Did you need anything, Shorty?"

I was on the fence. It could have been him. He had all the right parts.

"Uh, yeah. Have you ever been out Route 119 to this club?"

Levon wrinkled his brow, "Huh?"

"Uh, yeah. There's this club off the 119 called Cumberland Gap."

Levon looked genuinely puzzled. When he rinsed his hands, I saw a wedding ring on his left hand. "What sort of club is it, Shorty?"

I had to think fast. "Oh, see, I was gonna ask you the same thing because someone who looks a lot like you came out the other day while I was driving by."

"Couldn't have been me, Shorty. I never heard of the place."

"Well, I guess I'll have to go up there and just knock on the door."

Levon chuckled, "Careful. This county has a lot of dangerous people. Your club could be a front for racketeers or bootleggers."

So I had eliminated every possibility. I felt heartsick. Anytime I thought about sex with. Mr. Thick, it made my heart jump.

When the shift was over, I walked back to the trailer in a foul mood, taking inventory of my love life. I scared off the girl of my dreams. She rejected me so completely that I don't think I will ever be with a woman, baby or no baby. Frank, my Miner crush, was a jackass and a sadist. I couldn't get excited thinking about his big freckled cock and red pubes because he was a mean, awful person. Now the man I know only as Mr. Thick was haunting my daydreams and keeping me from focusing on my work. I had easy fucks like Moose and Willy, and I could have my pick of many of the miners in the showers. It was surprising how many married men would open their mouths or put their asses in the air for a shockingly huge cock like mine. But none of it meant anything unless my heart skipped a beat.

When I got home, I was glad to see the light was on in the trailer. I needed to talk to Earl, who was so easy to talk to and never judged me.

8

EARL

When I walked into the trailer, Earl was sprawled out in his underwear on the sofa, watching the tail end of a Creature Features about aliens who take over humans. They were called "body snatchers." Earl sat up, patted the sofa, and handed me a cold one. Together, we watched the human race come to an end.

During the final credits, Earl told me that it was a movie about communism disguised as science fiction. It made sense. That's the sort of stuff you learn in college.

Earl noticed right away that I was unhappy. "Shorty, what's eatin' ya?"

Good old Earl. He was a good listener and smart as a whip.

"It's a long story, Earl, but it starts at a club off the 119 called "Cumberland Gap.""

Earl nodded and let me continue.

"It's, um, a place for guys sort of like me to get together."

Earl surprised me, "A leather club, motorcycles."

"Yeah!" I guess they teach you a lot in college. "How did you know that?"

"Continue with your story, Shorty."

"Well, this fucking handsome asshole takes me

there. He's a sadist. He kept hurting me. I mean, some of it I liked, but mostly it made me feel like a slave or a dog."

Earl nodded. "Sounds degrading."

"Yeah, it was. He fucked me good, but it wasn't something I wanted again."

"Why did he take you to the club?"

I stopped to think. "I'm not sure, Earl; I think it was for the humiliation."

"What humiliation?"

"He cuffed me to a giant spiderweb made out of chains and pretty much just gave me to everyone in the room."

Earl didn't act surprised or judgmental. He just asked, "And was it humiliating?"

"Yes and no. I was ashamed of how much I enjoyed myself."

"So the whole thing was enjoyable?"

"Not the pinching and punching, but most of the rest was tolerable, and some stuff was so good, I can't stop thinking about it."

Earl nodded, so I explained it to him. "It turns out that despite having the biggest fuckpole in Harlan County, I like taking men's dicks inside me just as much, if not more, than fucking other men."

Earl asked, "Is there something wrong with that?"

I had to consider it. "I guess not, but I feel ashamed about how much I like it."

"You have nothing to be ashamed of. The pursuit of happiness is your right as an American."

Earl was right. I wasn't telling him the real bummer. He sensed there was more.

"Yeah, Earl, the part that makes me sad has to do with one man."

"Just one? Out of two dozen?"

I nodded. "He knew me, but I don't know who he was because I couldn't see him."

Earl smiled, "Well, if you know him, won't you eventually cross paths?"

"Yeah, but my heart aches for this guy. I know, it's stupid--"

"Hey! Nothing is stupid in affairs of the heart."

"I don't know who he is."

"Not the slightest clue? Did he say anything to you?"

"Other than that he knows me, no."

Earl asked, "You don't remember him telling you that he was a pig and you were his slop?" A wicked glint appeared in Earl's eyes.

My jaw dropped. "That was you?"

"Finally! I thought you were never going to figure it out!" Earl grabbed his cock through his underwear and squeezed it. "It's been torture for me ever since you showed me your colossal dick, Shorty."

I was struck dumb. I had lived with this man for nearly two years and always assumed he liked women, like his wife, Jody. But you can like both, and he does. I needed to say something.

"You fucked me so good, I can't stop thinking about it."

"I hope you'll return the favor." He stood up and yanked off his underwear, revealing his fat cock. It was as big around as mine, but not as long. As he got fully hard, it was even a little chubbier than mine, and it gained an inch in length.

But he did an about-face and kneeled on the sofa, holding his perfectly round white buttocks at waist level. He handed me a tub of Vaseline.

I put two fingers into the tub of petroleum jelly. One finger I wiped on my cock, and the other I stuck up Earl's ass.

After my finger had spread the lubricant thoroughly around the interior of Earl's beautiful ass, I took it out and used my whole hand to spread the jelly up and down my cock. It wasn't enough, so I went back for seconds until my whole cock was slick.

I leaned forward, pressing my cockhead into Earl's tight anus. He shuddered, but he didn't express any pain, so I pushed further. The petroleum jelly by itself wasn't reducing friction enough. Earl whispered, "Use your spit."

That whisper was the one I missed, the one that left me feeling empty in its absence. I pulled my slick cock out, spit in my hand a few times, then put a good helping of saliva at the entrance to Earl's anal cavity. What remained I spread up and down the length of my dick. I spit twice more for good measure, so my cock was extremely slippery. The combination of spit and Vaseline was ideal. My whole cock slipped in and stopped at the back of Earl's rectum. He pounded the sofa in pain.

"Should I stop?"

"Hell no! Fuck me!"

Earl had already visited my second room, so he knew what came next. I found the doorway and stretched it open. Earl cried out in pain, then quieted. I pushed through until I felt my balls bang into his. I put one hand on his gloriously thick dick and stroked it softly while I slammed my pubic mound into his butt crack.

With the agility of an acrobat, Earl swung his legs and rotated on my cock until he was facing me. He wrapped his legs around my waist and rapidly pulled me closer again and again so I was penetrating him as far as possible, then easing back. The back-and-forth motion felt good, as did the intimacy of his legs wrapped around my waist, but what felt best was leaning forward and giving Earl a deep tongue kiss. While I pistoned in and out of him, sometimes pounding against his rectum when I missed the doorway, we kissed passionately. Earl jerked his huge sausage cock, his knuckles brushing my hairless belly.

The kiss was steeped in more than just sex. It was a kiss of sexual passion, and it was a romantic kiss. Earl used one hand to play gently with my nipples. It caused me to shudder in extreme desire.

We stopped kissing for a moment, looking into each other's eyes. Earl said it first. "Shorty, I love you."

"Earl, I love you too."

The sex ascended to an entirely different plane. Instead of two grunting animals filling a basic need for sex, we were two humans, forming a lasting bond through mutual pleasure.

Earl showed me how to sit so he could straddle me and ride me like the big horse I was. He planted his feet on the floor and squatted down hard on my dick, taking it all the way. I felt my cock push its way into his guts, then slide out as he straightened his legs, only to let gravity take over, plunging downward, impaling himself. We fell into a rhythmic dance. I pushed my hips skyward to meet his descending butt and pulled away as he lifted himself skyward. I put my strong hands on his ass and helped him to lift off.

"That's it, Shorty, all the way out, all the way in!"

I pounded deep with each downstroke.

Earl groaned with pleasure. I stretched my neck to meet his lips, and we formed that electrical circuit again. It traveled like a current through a battery, negative to positive, ass to cock, lips and tongues entwined. And sealing the circuit was the love we professed for one another.

All the sex I had with other men had been about my own gratification. It was a race to the finish line. With Earl, it felt so different. I could only feel pleasure by giving it. His soft skin responded to my calloused hands by sending strong waves of pleasure back to me, which is how I knew he liked the feel of my touch. He wanted me all the way out and all the way in. I could only experience sexual pleasure by fulfilling his wishes. And so my cock made the long journey from sphincter past the rectum to the colon, and back out again, so that only my fat cock head remained inside, then all the way in, harder, faster as his ass set the pace. As he rode me like a pony, his own fat cock slapped me in the abdomen. I lowered my head and put his cock in my mouth. It tasted sweet, like cinnamon toast. It brought him even more pleasure, which I felt travel into me from his fat dick to my hungry tongue.

The flow of pleasure was additive. Each new sensation was added to a buildup of previously shared pleasures. As the pile grew, so did our electrical charge. Sparks flew as I repeatedly penetrated Earl, licked him, sucked him, stroked his nipples.

Without warning, I felt my balls contract, ready to release my come.

"Shit, Earl, I'm gonna come!"

He put his wrists on my shoulders to steady himself and doubled down, flying up and down the length of my cock with wild abandon. "Come inside me, Shorty!"

The contractions in the muscles at the base of my cock began slowly and increased to a frenzy. I pumped load after load of come into Earl. His insides were glazed with my sperm. He stood up, releasing my cock from his flesh tunnel. A steady trickle of my own come dripped onto my lap and into my cupped hand.

I used it to lubricate my asshole and spread the rest up and down the length of Earl's long fat cock.

In one swift movement, Earl pushed me back on the couch and lifted my ankles to his shoulders. He entered me immediately, plunging past my rectum. My whole ass was filled with his fat cock. It burned for a moment, but within moments, the pain was replaced with the joyful tingle of profound sensual delight. The delight came from Earl, who was rippling through the contours of my insides, feeling intense satisfaction on top of the anal pleasure he had just enjoyed from me. He pressed my knees up to my ears so my hole was trapped open for Earl to plunder. I could see his thick meat entering and exiting my hole. Knowing how good it felt for him made it feel even better for me. Earl was pumping rapidly, pounding my guts with brutal abandon. He lifted my hard cock and put it in his mouth. He sucked it like a jawbreaker, rolling it in his mouth from side to side. My cock was so long he found it easy to take it deep, past his tonsils. The sensation of my cock head rubbing against the sides of his throat took me to a new level of sexual enjoyment. To fill Earl's throat while he filled my ass got me very aroused.

Earl had been on the verge of orgasm the whole time I had been fucking him, so I was not surprised to feel him approaching climax.

I grabbed his ass cheeks and pushed him as far into me as he would go. I was stretched like a summer sausage casing. He held my cock deep in his throat and bobbed his head, pushing me over the edge.

"Oh fuck, Earl, you're gonna make me come again!"

But he knew that because he was right there. Just as I let loose a torrent of sperm into Earl's gullet, he painted my bowels with his sticky white goo. When Earl released my cock from his mouth, no sperm appeared. He had taken me so deep it shot directly down his throat into his stomach.

Earl was still rock-hard inside me, and I wondered if he needed to go again. I tweaked a nipple, and he flexed deep inside me. I wanted him to go again. I began squeezing his cock at the base with my anus.

As Earl began to fuck me again, his cock displaced his last load of come, and it dripped out of my hole. I caught some with my hand and tasted it. It was like the glaze on a cinnamon roll. He tasted like dessert.

By now, his girth and powerful strokes became an

easy, familiar sensation. Taking him completely sent waves of gratification throughout my body. I was in a state of perfect contentment; he could keep doing this for hours. Pain was in the past.

Earl was pumping in and out of me at a breakneck pace, his own come from earlier reducing the friction to allow for easy motion.

Earl was taller than me, but I hadn't realized just how strong his arms were until he picked me up and carried me around the room. I wrapped my legs around his waist, supported by his hips and muscular thighs. We locked lips and let our tongues explore each other. I tasted traces of my own semen in his mouth; it made me excited. My cock came to attention, sandwiched between our bellies.

Earl felt it, and when he looked, I felt him grow excited inside me.

"Damn, Shorty, are you gonna shoot a third time?"

I didn't answer him, although I suspected it might be the case. Instead, I put my tongue down his throat to taste more of my load in there.

Earl set me down on his bed, his cock still deeply embedded inside me. He rolled me onto my side, holding my right leg skyward. He was penetrating me from behind, but on the side. It changed the angle of his fucking so that he really scraped his way through my guts. It felt like heaven.

From this angle, he could get deeper than before. My second door was squashed, but he was pushing past it vigorously. It sent out pain signals, but they were canceled by the signals I got from Earl's happy cock.

In this position, I could easily rub my hand up and down my shaft. It felt too good not to, so I jacked myself fast and hard.

Earl moaned. It was time. He was going to shoot more milky semen into me. His buildup to orgasm was contagious; I felt my huge cock preparing for another blast.

In moments, Earl's breaths grew shallow. The added pressure from my squashed rectum must have helped a lot. "Oh, oh, Shorty, I'm gonna fucking come again. Are you ready?"

"Ready," I croaked, feeling an intense pressure as his cock grew thicker inside me.

He let out a yell and plunged deep inside me. I felt his huge cock head gushing male fluid in my colon. It put me over the top, and I shot a third load onto my face and upper body. Earl bent and licked a puddle from the base of my neck.

With Earl still buried inside me, I put my leg down and spooned. Earl softened, but he stayed inside me. He put an arm around me and kissed the back of my neck.

When I awoke in the morning, Earl was still in me. We had stayed joined all night.

As he stirred, I felt a rush of blood fill his piss-proud cock. We were going to have sex for breakfast, and I couldn't wait!

EPILOGUE

My split schedule gave me the time I needed to pass my equivalency and start attending Southeastern Technical Community College. I studied Anatomy and Biology, which is why I can tell you what was going where, and English, which is why I know some pretty big words now.

I moved into Earl's room, and we kept my bedroom as an office. Earl was a passionate lover. We spent many hours in bed discovering new ways to make each other feel good. He wasn't jealous or possessive. He let me earn my tips in the shower changing rooms. It paid for books and trips to big cities.

With Earl's contributions we were able to save enough to put a down payment on a house.

Leaving the trailer where we'd fallen in love and had explored each other's deepest recesses was a bittersweet parting. The new house up on a hill overlooked the Cumberland River and the Blue Ridge Mountains.

With my anatomy degree, I got a scholarship to the University of the Cumberlands in Pre-Med. I will graduate in a few months. With my good grades, I was accepted into Med School at Georgetown with a full scholarship. I'll go there in the Fall, but only if Earl moves there with me. He works in government already.

D.C. has more government jobs than it has people, so I know he'll do it. Besides, he's addicted to fucking me. He can't get enough. He can't fall asleep unless his dick is inside me or mine is in him. To tell you the truth, I can't either.

Working as a hurrier in a coal mine builds character in some and destroys it in others. I missed out on so much of life while spending my time underground. I was inhibited and had no sense of direction. Coming above ground to work in the showers was the catalyst that drove me to better myself. Being around so many naked men, I couldn't believe they were paying me to have that much fun. But now I see an even brighter future as a doctor. And I have a good man to share that future with. Love burns brighter than coal.

ABOUT THE AUTHORS

Peter Schutes is the nom de plume of a prolific and acclaimed novelist. As Peter Schutes, he is the author of Adult Erotic Fiction such as <u>The Slaves of Rome</u>, <u>Dark as a Dungeon</u>, <u>The Gospel of Priapus</u>, and <u>Panama Heat</u>. He writes in the style of vintage pulp authors from the 1960s and 1970s. He lives in Los Angeles.

Adam Maxwell Bigglesworth is the pen name of an aristocratic one-time heir to the throne of Scotland and a literary novelist.

Adam is the author of many novellas and short stories, including <u>Chopper Jock</u>, and <u>Satan's Sissy Boy</u>. Although his family lives in the Midlands of England, his roots are on the Isle of Lewis in the Outer Hebrides.

OTHER BOOKS FROM PETER SCHUTES PUBLISHING

Please visit Peter's Website to find links to all of Peter's books.

E-books and Paperbacks

The Able Seaman

The Anaconda Copper

The Autobiography of Peter Schutes

Backwoods Delivery

Big Bodies of All Sizes

Big Hole River

Bobbing Buoys and Salty Seamen

Buck Private

Bunkhouse Buddies

The Butt Baby

Chopper Jock

Cloistered

Coached

Confessions of a Rodeo Clown

Dark as a Dungeon

Demonic Deception *aka* Deceived, Cursed & Blessed

Desert Island Daddies

Dirty Dorms and Fresh Men

Dutch Treat

The Expectant Member

Firehouse Lovers

The Fish

Five Erotic Tales
The Gospel of Priapus
Hercules and Lippos
Hobo Honey
Hoboes, Hustlers, and Outlaws
Hot Blue Collars
Hotshot
Like the Greeks Do
Little Shamus
Logger's Delight
Muscle Bottom
Panama Heat
Satanic Seductions
Satan's Sissy Boy
The Slaves of Rome
Small Cockpits and Big Hangars
The Spotter
Steroid Steve
The Thigh Baby
Under the Boardwalk
Wee Dobbin
World's Biggest

***** Coming Soon *****
Cosmic Cage: Gay SF Erotica
Tales of Two Daddies
More Tales of Two Daddies
Mowing and Blowing